PENGUIN BOOKS

TOKYO WOES

Bruce Jay Friedman is the author of, among others, *Stern*, *A Mother's Kisses*, *The Lonely Guy's Book of Life*, *Let's Hear It for a Beautiful Guy*, the plays *Steambath* and *Scuba Duba*, the screenplay *Stir Crazy*, and co-author of the award-winning screenplay *Splash!* He makes his home in Water Mill, New York.

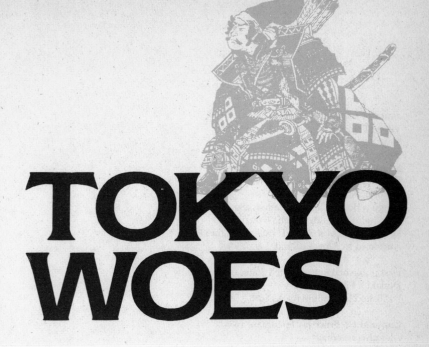

TOKYO WOES

Bruce Jay Friedman

Penguin Books

PENGUIN BOOKS

Viking Penguin Inc., 40 West 23rd Street,
New York, New York 10010, U.S.A.
Penguin Books Ltd, Harmondsworth,
Middlesex, England
Penguin Books Australia Ltd, Ringwood,
Victoria, Australia
Penguin Books Canada Limited, 2801 John Street,
Markham, Ontario, Canada L3R 1B4
Penguin Books (N.Z.) Ltd, 182–190 Wairau Road,
Auckland 10, New Zealand

First published in the United States of America by
Donald I. Fine, Inc., 1985
Published in Penguin Books 1986

LIBRARY OF CONGRESS CATALOGING IN PUBLICATION DATA
Friedman, Bruce Jay, 1930–
Tokyo woes.
I. Title.
PS3556.R5T6   1986   813'.54   85-31048
ISBN 0 14 00.8705 2

Printed in the United States of America by
R.R. Donnelley & Sons Company, Harrisonburg, Virginia
Set in Palatino

TOKYO WOES

TOKYO WOES

THE FLIGHT

MIKE HALSEY woke up a little earlier than usual, probably in response to the harsh cackle of a nearby possum. It seemed to be exulting in the fact that it was—verifiably—the only such creature in the county. Once he was up, Mike knew he didn't stand much chance of ducking back into a good sleep again. He didn't have that knack. So he slipped quietly out of bed and yanked off his nightgown. He had never imagined he would wind up as a nightgown person, but Pam had given him a red flannel one for his birthday and he now had them in four different colors. Mike felt that a nightgown certainly did give you a free and easy sensation—although he did notice that he would yank his off the minute he got up. He rinsed off his contact lenses and, once again, promised himself to get the kind that stayed in for a full month—so that you could charge out of bed and confront intruders.

With his eyesight all set, he stood back and marveled at Pam. He did this even though her breathing was a little thick and snuffly and she didn't hit her stride in the beauty department until she was a little deeper into the day. After she had poured down a few cups of coffee.

Then you could really see those cheekbones. Pam had put on a little weight, which didn't concern him much since he was confident she would know when to hit the brakes in that department. Hell, look at his own belly. What was it, a washboard? Besides, they lived way out in the country, so what difference did a couple of pounds make. In the city, he might have had a word with her about it. But out in the woods and under the covers, it fell into the category of generalized coziness. And when she nestled that warm tush back up against him, he didn't have a worry in the world. What a wiggler. She'd been wiggling when he met her and as proof of her integrity, she was wiggling five years later.

She had gotten into a second bottle of wine the night before and showed no signs of any imminent activity that could be considered serious. He'd forgotten what it was, but she had found something to celebrate. So he decided to tiptoe out and round up the papers, so that they would be all set for her when she started her day. Pam had majored in international monetary law, but she went crazy over the gossip columns and loved to holler out items to him about the latest activities of people like Barbara de Portago and Chessy Rayner. He would counter with a Cher tidbit. He and Pam were great pals and matched up pretty well in bed. But they often speculated that it was their fierce love of column items that kept them together.

Downstairs, he started up a fire in the wood stove, even though, strictly speaking, it wasn't necessary. He just liked to make wood-stove fires. Now that he had mastered them. And besides, this particular stove had cost a lot of money to install. Whenever Pam asked him why he was making a wood-stove fire he would say: "I just want to dry out the air a little."

He fed Mort some Cycle Three dog food, although, once again, strictly speaking, he should have had him on Four, the final cycle. He certainly was glad they didn't have cycle food for people. That's all he would have needed—a daily reminder of what cycle he was on. He let the big guy out for a quick romp around the grounds and then hopped into his wagon and headed for the Redneck Deli.

At the edge of the driveway, he checked to see if the sign was in place. When they had taken possession of the house, that was the first thing they had gotten, a sign that said: Halsey/Levine. They had then pounded it in—after first flipping to see whose name got on there first. On this particular morning, the sign was exactly where it belonged. An old man who lived nearby had been yanking it out at night. He was under the impression that it belonged to a real estate shark who was out to carve up the area into condominiums. Mike had explained that he and Pam were his neighbors and that the sign was just to indicate that they lived there. But they couldn't get through to the old-timer who kept yanking it out in the dead of night—although not as often. So Mike would just patiently stick it back in. The old man couldn't possibly have that much further to go, although people tended to live forever in that area. Compared to everyone else, he and Pam were pups.

The Redneck, which was run kind of casually, had a sign

in the window that said it wouldn't be open until three in the afternoon—since it was Good Friday. Actually, there weren't any rednecks at the deli, but the first time Pam and Mike walked into the store, a free-for-all had broken out between some fellows who claimed they had been charged the previous day for lettuce and tomatoes on their sandwiches and hadn't gotten any—and the owners who said they certainly had. Bodies flying all over the place because of lettuce and tomatoes. So the Redneck seemed like the right name for the place. Actually, it was just a deli frequented by high-paid construction workers who got their breakfast and lunch there. As a fellow who restored houses, Mike knew many of them.

He decided to head for yet another deli some ten minutes away. He had a vague notion it sold newspapers, too. And he knew how much those column items meant to Pam.

Normally, Mike was a fellow who liked to stay close to his beat. Once he bought newspapers in one place, that's where he bought them. He had seen the same dentist since he was a youngster and continued to do so even though Dr. Newman was pushing eighty and had to bring in a special man to give novocaine injections. So he wouldn't drill through somebody's cheek. Mike was a fellow who kept to the center of the road, although he had to admit that every time he swerved off a bit it had worked out nicely. Going after Pam, for example, when she was supposed to be living with an ornithologist. Some instinct told him to jump over a juice bar at a health food store to get at her. And to follow her to Nova Scotia when she was confused and couldn't make up her mind about him and was trying to lose herself in novels about the British gentry. That had certainly worked out. Or how about giving up sixteen years of middle management security and going off to restore houses with a short gay guy named Rick. A fellow he had met in Dr. Newman's office. That was quite a little swerve.

And yet it still seemed adventurous to buy the papers in a new place.

The diner that he remembered only vaguely was all boarded up, so he decided to press on and look for yet another paper store. This was getting out of hand. Not that he had to worry about a wide-awake Pam. She had really gone to town on the wine and if he knew that rascal she was good for a whole morning's worth of z's. Realistically speaking, he was looking at early afternoon. But why disturb old prettyface. Would she wake him up in a similar situation? Forget it.

Going a little further involved taking an unfamiliar lakeside road. A real escalation for Mike. The experience, everyday stuff for most people, got him both shaky and excited at the same time. It was like running around naked. The heavily wooded lakeside road went spiraling off to nowhere and he sensed that he was not going to run into any paper stores along the way. Yet he kept driving. Maybe he was wrong and he would pass some kind of general supply store for trappers. One with sticks of pepperoni in cellophane and a few papers.

A couple of carved signposts indicated the area had once been inhabited by Indians. Some probably lived there still. That in itself interested Mike only slightly, but a grouping of bewitched little cabins, set back in a glade, caught his attention. He wondered who lived in them and what it would be like to buy one suddenly, move into it and not tell anyone, not even Pam. And start living there as a whole new person. The thought got his blood pumping. His heart seemed to move toward his throat and he felt as if his legs had developed springs. Uh oh, he said, here

I go again. The wind sweeping off the lake made him feel
dizzy and elated. It was all he could do to keep from flying
out of his seat. He gripped the wheel so hard he almost
broke it, but there was no way to calm himself down. Even
pulling over to the side and thinking things over didn't
help. The last time he got a similar feeling he wound up
on the coast of Finland. He had not been living with Pam
then. He had been living with a garment center model.
But the experience had taught him always to keep an up-
to-date passport in the glove compartment. This time he
headed for Japan.

MIKE LETS PAM KNOW WHAT HE'S UP TO

THE FIRST thing he did when he arrived at San Francisco Airport was to call Pam.

"Where ya at, babe?" she said, with a yawn. "The Redneck?"

"No, I'm in San Francisco."

"Whatcha doin' there, hon?" He could tell she was rubbing her eyes and looking around for a cigarette.

"I'm on my way to Japan."

"Japan," she said, still a little foggy. "Are you all right?"

"I'm fine, hon. This feeling came over me suddenly and I thought I better go with it. You know those feelings."

"I sure do, hon," she said. "Do you have clothes and things? Let me get a cigarette."

When she got back on, he told her that all he had with him for the moment were the things he was wearing. But that he would pick up a few items at the airport.

"I thought I'd just play it by ear."

"Why'd you pick Japan, Mike? Wasn't it Prague you were curious about?"

She was probably on her feet now, looking at the bay to see if she could figure out what kind of day it would be. They weren't on the bay, but they were close enough to check the current for any kind of roughness in the weather.

"I wasn't that interested in Prague, Pam. I was for a *while*, but then it faded out on me. It was always Japan."

"Well, hon," she said with another yawn, a full-out variety this time. "I got to hand it to you. You sure do act on those feelings of yours. Do you have any idea when you'll be back?"

"I don't want to set a tight time schedule, hon. That would spoil the whole thing."

"You're not gonna *live* there, are you, Mike?"

She said it with a kind of playful panic. He could see her eyes dancing as she acted horrified. What a little performer. He felt like biting her ass.

"Pam," he said, coming in with a dramatic sigh of his own.

"All right," she said, changing direction. "I just wanted to make sure. I do not want to lose my fella. Now promise me one thing. That you'll take *very very* good care of yourself. Mort and I will be fine. And we love you, you great big goof."

"I love you, too, hon. And for God's sake, don't worry about me. I'll be fine."

"I know, babe. Did you get the papers?"

"Not really," he said, steeling himself. "It was Good Friday."

"Wait a minute, wait a minute," she said, as if reeling in disbelief and trying to collect herself. "I just want to make sure I heard you correctly. You didn't get the *papers?*" She was awake now. Oh boy, was she awake.

"The stores were closed," he said weakly.

"I don't believe this, Mike. How could you do a thing like that. You know how much those papers mean to me."

"Of course I do," he said. "And there's a strong chance you can get them now. Otherwise, I never would have pulled out this way. But don't do this to me, Pam. Don't send me off like this."

"All right, I won't," she said. "Because believe it or not, I really do love you.

"But I just don't *see* how a person can go to Japan and not get the goddamned papers."

"HI, I'M WILLIAM (CALL ME BILL) ATENABE"

HE FELT a lot better after he had spoken to Pam. And except for the bumpy part at the end, he felt it had gone quite well. Not that he was surprised. He had picked himself quite a honey. He thought of her trooping downstairs in her nightgown, still rubbing her eyes, and wished he could have been there to come up behind her and slip his hands over those heavy jugs. She'd say *Mi-i-i-i-ke* and try to slap his hands and wiggle away, which would only get him crazier. Next thing you know they'd be rolling around on the floor without the faintest idea of which one got them started. And they would have this cozy, absolutely secure sex, maybe not wild by other people's standards—

21

there was no need to dress up in squaw costumes—but perfectly satisfactory to him, with Pam digging in her heels and slapping him like he was a horse, and him feeling like king of the world and always sneaking looks at her mischievous face. They were some team. And then they would have a huge breakfast, making vows not to have another one like it for a month. So that they could both get skinny once and for all. Sometimes, they would even *discuss* the breakfasts during a so-called lull in the proceedings.

He worried about Pam being alone in the woods at night, but if he had mentioned that on the phone, he was sure she would have said: "What's wrong with Mort? Don't I have Mort?" The big guy would react to a leaf falling in the next county, but neither one of them knew for sure how he would respond to real trouble. Mike wasn't ready to bet the family jewels on it, but he had a feeling that the playful F.A.O. Schwartz-style pup would do just fine. He might even tear out a throat for himself.

Mike kept a signed check in his desk drawer to cover all emergencies. She knew where it was and that all she had to do was cart it over to the bank and she would be set for a while. But if he knew his sweet potato, she probably wouldn't even cash it and would work with the money she had picked up doing freelance carpentry. He thought of Pam in a pair of coveralls—that tush—and decided he had better get off the subject fast. Or he might just turn around.

It occurred to Mike that he should probably get in touch with his partner Rick and tell him he was off to Japan, but he decided Pam would be ahead of him on that score. In any case, Rick would probably just shake his head and do his spooky smile. He was one spooky little guy, with a big brush mustache covering his mouth so that you could never quite tell what he was thinking. You had to work with his eyes. But he was a good partner and he had never tried any of that gay stuff on Mike. Only once had he even come close to trying some. He was showing Mike how to strip down a brass lighting fixture and when Mike thanked him, Rick said he could show Mike "lots of things." His eyes were leaping all over the place when he said that, even though he pretended to be fixing his awl. But that was about it. That was the most suggestive he had ever been in their entire work relationship.

As far as Mike could tell, he was all set to go to Japan.

He had never been to the country, of course, and he had no idea of how he would do over there, but he was certainly anxious to give it a try. And he wasn't terribly worried about it, either. Take the language barrier. From what he had heard, they hardly even bothered to speak Japanese over that way. Except on formal occasions. Or if they lived in the backwoods. He heard they spoke a little in country inns.

He didn't know a soul in Japan unless you wanted to count the professor who somehow had gotten the impression that Mike had restored a house for Dizzy Gillespie. They'd exchanged a few letters but the correspondence petered out quickly. Mike had no desire to visit him, although he was sure the fellow would have been happy to show him around. Mike didn't even like sushi that much. He had been to a Kurosawa Festival and stayed for about three-quarters of it. No rap on the great filmmaker, but one offering seemed to blend into the next. Mike saluted Japan's technological mastery, along with everyone else, but none of it meant very much to him unless it translated down to some delicious little gadget he could fool around with. Something you could wear on your wrist that told you the weather.

Yet this is the country he was drawn to.

He was anxious to stay at one of those "mail-slot" hotels where they slip you into a little squared-off compartment for the night and then come get you in the morning. Supposedly, you had all your needs taken care of in there. They furnished you with teeny little bathroom conveniences and tricky little entertainment mechanisms, many of which had yet to make their appearance in the States. And there was a breakfast lounge for fellows who had spent the night in slots, and who had presumably developed a feeling of solidarity. Mike just hoped they had slots that were big enough for him. It was no exaggeration to say that he was a big strapping fellow.

He bought some sundries, congratulating himself along the way for remembering to pick up a hair dryer, an item he always forgot to take along on trips. It occurred to him that he was now the proud owner of four hair-dryers, although this last one had a new wrinkle: it was flat-shaped and you could carry it in your back pocket. It was made by the Japanese people. In a way, it would give him a head start on Japan.

He and Rick had done so well restoring houses that American Express had awarded them both gold credit cards. It was this card that he used to purchase a round-trip ticket to Japan with an open return. He thought of himself as a regular fellow and something of a humanist, but he had to admit he enjoyed being one of the Americans that Amex had chosen to put in this select group. Not that he walked up to the counter and slapped the card down in triumph. The Japanese airline personnel had been around for too many years and seen too many gold cards to get bowled over by one that was signed Mike Halsey. But he did enjoy sliding it over to them.

He decided to go first class. As long as he was doing it,

why not do it right? Which, incidentally, was the slogan he and Rick used for their business. He could always tighten up and go tourist on the way back. Once he was on the plane and saw all the extra leg room he had gotten, he knew he had made the right choice. He immediately took advantage of it, stretching his legs out as far as they could go and enjoying a feeling of well-being. But when the plane lifted off, he suddenly realized that he was going to be nine thousand miles away from Pam and Mort and their beautiful home. This gave him an anxiety attack. He gripped both arm rests and felt his body rise up as if he were a parade float. He knew what those attacks were like. Once they got started, it would take half a dozen Japanese guys to hold him down. Not that the other passengers were little fellows. They were a lot less short and squat than he had imagined. As a matter of fact, there were a couple of genuine beanpoles on board. No doubt they lived in cosmopolitan areas.

The stewardess offered him a glass of water, which was helpful. She tilted her wafer-thin face up at him and it was like looking at a plate of ham and eggs. The last time he had seen a face like that was on a vase in his aunt's house. It was a little too Japanese-looking for his taste and he hoped they had other kinds of women over there. Not that he was looking for women. Who would with a little sweetheart like Pam waiting back home?

Thinking about the stewardess with the pan face took Mike's mind off his troubles and before he knew it, his anxiety attack had subsided. To be on the safe side, he decided to throw some water on his face. Standing in the aisle, next to the john, was a stocky, pleasant-looking fellow in a windbreaker. He had his hands in his pockets and was a little slouched over, like a coach on the sidelines.

There was no question that he was Japanese, although Mike felt there might have been someone from Illinois in the picture as well. Mike guessed he was about his own age—mid to late thirties. He seemed like the kind of fellow Mike could get along with. A regular guy. They smiled at each other and went into a series of mutual bows, indicating it didn't matter who went to the john first. Mike hadn't been the least bit worried about getting the hang of bowing, and as it turned out, he was right. After they had both used the john, they met again in the aisle and smiled at one another.

"Are you traveling on business or pleasure?" the fellow asked, breaking the ice conversationally. He had the nicest way of speaking with only the faintest touch of a Japanese accent humming away in the background.

"Quite frankly," said Mike, "I'm not sure."

With a sly wink and an affectionate punch on the shoulder—he'd obviously spent time in the States—the fellow said he knew exactly what he meant, which of course he couldn't possibly have since Mike himself wasn't sure what he was getting at. Mike returned the affectionate punch on the shoulder, the way fellows will do when they're feeling each other out. They proceeded to exchange a few more affectionate punches, which seemed like the most natural thing in the world to be doing. But then the stewardess asked them if they would please return to their seats. They decided to take two empty ones that were side by side. After a brief misunderstanding about who got to use the center arm rest, one that was quickly resolved, Mike's new friend introduced himself as William (call me Bill) Atenabe. He said he worked for a large Japanese company and had been sent to America to study corporate athletic programs. The next thing Mike knew, Bill, as if to demonstrate, had jumped out in the aisle and was squatting down, pounding an imaginary catcher's mitt.

"Way to go, fella," he said, as if encouraging a pitcher. "This sucker can't hit. Gimme some smoke."

The stewardess asked Bill if he would please return to his seat and try to restrain himself. Mike was a fan of the New York Islanders hockey team, but chuckled all the same at Bill's baseball lingo.

"You're the first Japanese fellow I've ever met," he told Bill, "and I'm delighted you turned out to be such a swell guy."

"You're a nice guy, too," said Bill, chucking Mike on the arm. Mike returned the compliment and they would have been at it again if Mike hadn't noticed a small wiry Japanese old-timer next to him, blowing cigarette smoke in his face.

"Knock it off," said Mike.

In response, the man, who had a close-cropped military-style haircut, waved an arm at him in a threatening manner and took a few quick spiteful puffs in Mike's direction.

"Now look," said Mike, who was about to grab the fellow and put an end to his rudeness.

But his friend Bill interceded, saying something to the man which caused him to back off—although not until he had gotten in one last puff and another hostile arm wave.

Bill said the fellow was his father, Poppa Kobe, and to please try not to mind him.

"He held out in the jungles of the Philippines for two years after the war ended," said Bill, "and frankly, he's still a little anti-American.

"Not only that," said Bill, "but when he finally came out, nobody particularly cared. It was only years later that the people of his village, out of shame, gave him a little parade."

Adding insult to injury, said Bill, his father, who had

been a director of one of Japan's leading companies, was now being forcibly retired. Already, a "brain-squeezer" from Todai University had been dispatched to his home to extract all of the expertise that Poppa Kobe had stored up in his years at the company—for deposit in a company wisdom bank.

"Once she finishes up," said Bill, "it looks like noodle-time for poor Poppa Kobe."

He explained that for his father, as with other workers in the same age category, the opening of a noodle shop was all that lay open to him upon retirement.

"And how many noodle shops can the country take?" asked Bill, which Mike thought was an excellent question.

Thus far, Poppa Kobe, a proud and self-sufficient type, had resisted that option, although he had looked at a few sites on an informal basis.

"So take it easy on the guy," said Bill. "He's a good skate when you get to know him."

"You got it," said Mike. By tacit agreement, both men conceded that they were exhausted and decided it was time to take a nap.

Bill dropped off first and was soon snoring up a storm. It was impossible for Mike to get annoyed at him. He was a lot like "Doggie," Mike's childhood friend, so nicknamed for his way of sticking his tongue out and panting after a ballgame. Someone told Mike that Doggie had become a nurse, which was disconcerting at first, although whatever Doggie wanted to do with his life was Doggie's business. The fact that Mike had marked him down for construction was beside the point.

This was like being with a Japanese Doggie.

And Bill certainly did look a lot more Japanese when he slept, which was all right with Mike. It didn't interfere with his feelings for his new friend one bit. Bill's sleeping noises were hypnotic and before he knew it, Mike himself was out like a light. When they both awakened from re-freshing snoozes, Bill asked Mike where he planned to stay in Japan. Mike told him about the mail-slot hotels and Bill would have none of it, insisting that Mike stay with the Atenabes.

"We've got plenty of room by Japanese standards," said Bill, "and I won't have it any other way."

Mike put up a protest, although secretly he was de-lighted by the invitation. Who could pass up an invitation to stay in someone's cozy house instead of a hotel, even one that featured a fascinating mail-slot device and the latest in gadgetry? Especially in a strange land. And the Atenabes probably had some gadgets of their own, real practical ones that weren't just fly-by-night. Pam, too, would be relieved to learn that Mike had been seized up by a reliable fellow like Bill instead of wandering out anon-ymously into a generalized Japan.

"It's one of the nicest offers I've ever had," said Mike, "and I think I'll just take you up on it."

He beamed at Bill, and for his part Bill dropped down in his seat, pulling up the collar of his windbreaker—no doubt out of shyness.

Mike knew that Japan was more than a hop, skip and a jump away, but he hadn't thought through what ten hours on a plane would be like. It was something like a bus ride to Cincinnatti. You'd be on there for quite some time but not long enough to justify getting set up for a night's sleep. Mike had brought along a book about Car-dinal Richelieu that he had taken a few shots at before. He waded into it gamely once again, but did not have any more luck with it on this occasion. You had to know the whole period for Richelieu's role to click in properly. Other-wise, you were just kidding yourself. So he set the book aside and occupied himself with several stray but useful functions such as working on his nails so that they could be all trimmed up for his stay in Japan. Then he decided to thin down his wallet, getting rid of business cards that had been slipped to him by patio contractors late at night in bars. He knew down deep that he would never call those fellows.

Bill turned out to be an excellent traveling companion. He leaned across once or twice to make sure Mike didn't throw away anything important, but for the most part, he remained slouched down in his seat, lost in thought. He seemed to sense that Mike didn't want anyone jabbering in his ear any more than he wanted someone jabbering in his.

The two friends were served a substantial dinner that was split down the middle between Japanese offerings and Western ones, so as not to hurt anyone's feelings. When Mike had polished his off, he popped down a couple of brandies and adjusted his seat so that he could recline as far back as possible without crushing the fellow's knees behind him. He wondered what kind of dinner Pam would be having and guessed it would be a pair of bologna sandwiches. No doubt she had slapped together a few of them the minute she was confident he was safely on his way and couldn't catch her at it. With all the tasty and healthful concoctions that were available to her, even in his absence, he could not understand her passion for bologna sandwiches. He would have told her that if he were there. And she would have kept right on munching away, looking out over the top of the sandwich with her eyes sparkling, and possibly cramming in some potato chips, another favorite of hers. *Pam munching on a bologna sandwich*. There probably wasn't another soul who would see anything romantic in that picture. But they didn't know Pam. And the way she looked at Mike over the top of it. A dark thought suddenly took hold of him. What if something happened to her while he was away? He wondered if he could get along without her and decided that he definitely could not. He would go spinning out of control, like a machine with its wires loose, and tumble off a pier. Of course, Pam did believe in an afterlife and had pretty much convinced him that one existed. She had sold him on the idea that they could pick right up where they left off. This neatly solved the problem of what to do if one of them dropped out before the other. So Mike, after consideration, decided that if he lost Pam, he would probably be able to hold out for a while until they hooked up in the afterlife. Not that it would be any sleigh ride. But he would be able to wait it out. This was the drift of his thinking as he stared out at the Pacific and drew closer to his destination. He must have been daydreaming longer than he realized. The light had changed and he could have sworn he heard atonal Far Eastern music in the distance. The thought of how close he must be to Japan made his mouth water.

What seemed like a small insignificant chunk of an island slid by beneath them. But at the sight of it, Poppa Kobe jumped to his feet and hollered out *"Banzai,"* getting others around him to join in. A thin man in a starched collar flew at Bill's dad and tried to silence him by clamping a hand on his mouth. Poppa Kobe bit the fellow's fingers and shouted what seemed to be cursewords at him. Mike recognized one of the epithets as having been directed at him some hours before. After they had been separated by the hardworking stewardess and order had been restored, Bill explained that the atoll in question had once belonged to Japan; it was Poppa Kobe's feeling that it should be returned immediately since it was part of the empire. However trivial it appeared in size. The fellow who had attempted to silence Poppa Kobe was a member of the Diet, whose position was that Japan's future lay in technology—and not in worrying about every little atoll.

The issue was obviously an emotional one; even now, ten rows apart, the two adversaries continued to hiss and snarl at one another.

"What's that special cussword Poppa Kobe uses?" Mike wanted to know. "The one he directed at me as well."

Bill said that there weren't that many cusswords in the Japanese language and that the one Mike referred to was probably "radish-head."

"That isn't bad at all," said Mike.

"It's one of the worst we have," said Bill.

There was no question now that Japan was just around the corner. To celebrate, Mike suggested they have a brandy, totally miscalculating the effect it would have on Bill. All it took was one to send his friend twirling down the aisles, rotating his hips, shaking imaginary castanets over his head and singing "La Cucaracha." Several respectable-looking Japanese businessmen picked up Bill's cue and all hell broke loose. This time, the long-suffering stewardess simply threw up her hands and let her countrymen wail. The pilot finally restored some semblance of order with an announcement that the plane was getting ready to land. Like actors starting a new scene, the rowdy Japanese quietly returned to their seats. Mike looked out of the window and got his first look at Japan.

A COUNTRY UNLIKE ANY OTHER

IT WAS Japan all right, no doubt about it. It was unlike any other country Mike had ever seen. There were lonely mountains and fog and little patches of farmland and the choppy outlines of an industrial metropolis. All kind of scrambled together in a dreamy montage. Where the fog curled around the perfectly coned mountaintops, it was soft and dusky and tinted with a blue duotone. Mike felt there was power and delicacy and mischief out there, too. The mischief is what probably set it off from other countries. You could practically see those Shinto gods, racing around the edges of the mountains, tickling each others' feet, running and tripping and frolicking and shooting each other with bows and candied arrows. And if you

33

caught up with one and tried to consult him, he would say: "I'm afraid you have the wrong god." Because he would be too busy having fun.

Mike just about wept when he set eyes on Japan and knew he had come to the right place, even if it had seemed crazy to take off the way he did.

Preparations for landing began. Some of the passengers changed into Japanese-looking outfits, kimonos and such, but then, almost as an afterthought, got right back into their Western business suits. Bill just hung in there with his windbreaker, although he did break out a pair of sandals. Mike had the feeling it was because his feet hurt and not that it was any kind of cultural salute.

Lined up with his fellow passengers at the exit doors, Mike became aware of a strange smell that seemed to be indigenous to Japan. It wasn't sweat. Mike was now prepared to testify that these people did not sweat, or at least to the extent that had been commonly thought in the West. The fish diet had no doubt taken care of that. A slight smell of peanut oil was the most that could be laid at their doorstep. That and a tiny hint of burnt-out firecrackers. But who knows, maybe it was just the excitement of returning to their land.

The stewardess with the ham-and-eggs face began to sob quietly as the plane taxied toward the hanger.

"She sure does love it here," said Mike.

Bill corrected Mike's thinking a bit and told him that she did indeed love Japan but that she was crying because she felt she hadn't done a good enough job of serving the passengers.

"Those are tears of shame," said Bill.

"I think she did a good job," said Mike. "We were a little rambunctious back there, but it wasn't her fault. Tell her she has nothing to be ashamed of."

"She won't care," said Bill. "And besides, I agree with her."

Mike started a bit. It was the first time he and his friend had what amounted to even the slightest falling-out and he was a little thrown. What it taught him was that even though Bill wore an old windbreaker and reminded him of Doggie, Bill was *not* Doggie. Bill was Japanese, and as such, was subject to quirks. It didn't stop him from being a swell guy. It was just something to watch out for.

As they moved toward the terminal, it occurred to Mike for the first time that his preparations for the trip had been skimpy, to say the least. Japan did not seem like the kind of country that just let you walk right in. And all Mike had with him were his good intentions.

It was a lucky thing he had met Bill. Despite his new friend's casual dress and self-effacing manner, Mike had the feeling Bill came from a highborn and influential family. Bill confirmed the impression by slipping away for a moment, consulting with some government officials and then returning to say they were in good shape. All he needed to know was if Mike was a leper. Mike assured him he was not. Nor had there been any lepers in his family.

"Then we're all set," said Bill.

The two friends cleared Customs and Immigration without event and walked into a reception area where each passenger was given a standing ovation. Even Mike got a little round of applause, although clearly he stood apart from the returning Japanese. Poppa Kobe was swept off by a raucous and feisty little group of old-timers who, as Bill pointed out, were members of his old Pacific unit. Mike and Bill waited around for someone to pick them up, but soon were alone in the terminal.

"Oh well," said Bill, in a jaunty manner, "let's take the bus."

He tried to be matter-of-fact about it, but Mike could tell he was a little hurt.

Mike and Bill got into a crowded bus and were given oxygen masks by an attendant who was much prettier than the airline stewardess, at least by his standards. She didn't look quite so authentically Japanese, which was the part he wasn't ready for. He couldn't understand the masks—it wasn't as if they were at altitude and might suddenly go into a dive—but he readied himself to slap his on just in case. Maybe they just wanted you to have a little whiff of oxygen, on the house, like an aperitif. He didn't feel like asking Bill the answer to any of his questions. His friend had been a little gloomy ever since his disappointment at the arrival gate and Mike decided to give him some space.

The attendant took up a position next to the driver and told everyone in English and Japanese how many moving parts there were on the bus and how many times the wheels revolved per mile. She also filled in the group on how many buses the company owned and how many they were shooting for in the future. The last bit of information produced some oohs and aaahs in the crowd, but not from Mike. He was anxious to learn about Japan, but he did not see how he could throw this type of information into play. So he turned and stared out at the countryside. Gloomy industrial sites gave way to ancient rice paddies, which in turn gave way to apartment compounds just as he was about to settle in with the ancient rice paddies. The quick transitions got him dizzy and he could see that it was going to be tough to get a handle on Japan.

The ride seemed to take forever and just when Mike was about to give up on getting anywhere, the bus pulled into the second story of a department store. How it managed that trick was a mystery to Mike. Had the bus sprouted wings? In any case, there they were, in the shoe department of one of Japan's top shopping emporiums. Bill and Mike got out, along with half the passengers and the bus roared off, no doubt to deposit the rest of its complement high up in the grandstand of some ballpark.

ESCALATOR
MAYHEM

BILL SEEMED to know the way and led Mike into one of those celebrated human waves of Japanese shoppers, only a small minority of whom pointed at Mike, held their noses and called out: *Gaijin, gaijin."* Mike shouldered his way through in a good-natured way, but was ready to swat anyone who got too contentious.

Bill and Mike joined a column of shoppers who were waiting to get on an escalator. At the foot of it, a fellow in a stovepipe hat had dusted off each shopper before the individual stepped on and then dusted the escalator steps, although not as vigorously. When it was his turn, Mike let himself get dusted, then grabbed the duster and dusted the fellow right back. Confused at first, the attendant took back his duster and gave Mike a second going-over. Undismayed, Mike grabbed a mop and swatted the fellow with it a few times. The attendant tried to dust Mike right out of the store and by the time Bill realized what was happening it was too late to avoid a melee. He grabbed a whiskbroom and the three of them went at it, up and down the escalator stairs, whooping and hollering, not producing any real damage but giving the effect of a full-out riot. Actually, it was Mike who did the real hollering. Bill and the attendant's was kind of a polite internal hollering that you could sense rather than hear. All three tumbled off the escalator and rolled into the kimono department, the head of which came running out and begging them to please stop. The appearance of an executive sobered up the trio quickly; they got to their feet, huffing and puffing and straightening their clothes. With some formality, the executive handed his card to Bill, who glanced at it and then produced one of his own. The executive looked it over and seemed impressed. Then he turned to Mike, who pulled his pockets inside out to indicate that he did not carry a card. He had always left that kind of thing to his partner Rick, who had had some beautiful embossed ones made up. The executive, however, seemed to take Mike's cardless state as a personal affront and began to tremble with rage. Mike told Bill that his partner Rick was the one in charge of the cards and Bill, in turn, passed this information along to the executive, who seemed placated, but not entirely. The fellow in the stovepipe hat passed around a few of *his* cards, although no one in the group had particularly asked to see them. In among them were some porno pictures which Mike thought were inappropriate to the situation. The executive took another look at Bill's card as if to confirm what he'd seen the first time. Then he dismissed the attendant and took Bill and Mike on a first-class shopping tour of the store. The friends were treated with utmost courtesy, each item they handled having been dusted by a salesperson before they touched it, with no attempt to dust them. Mike picked up some socks and underwear and a couple of sweatsuits. He always liked to knock around in a sweatsuit, almost no matter where he was. Bill bought a surfboard and a full complement of scuba equipment.

Somehow Mike could not picture his friend hitting the top of the waves and Bill confessed that indeed he had never set so much as a toe in the ocean. But he loved sports equipment. The executive saw to it that each of their purchases was wrapped in a loving manner. The wrappings themselves were little works of art. Mike thought it was a shame to waste them on socks and T-shirts, but it was obviously not his dime, so he let them wrap away.

They thanked the store executive for his many courtesies, Mike following Bill's lead in saying good-bye with a bow. Once again, the executive flushed and balled up his fists in anger. Mike sensed that he was at fault and he was right on that score. Bill explained that Mike, innocently of course, had given the fellow a curt and formal bow of the type that generally terminated an acrimonious meeting.

"Try one of these," said Bill, demonstrating a light and friendly variety.

Mike imitated his friend—to the best of his ability—and was rewarded by a toothy grin on the part of the executive.

At the street level, Mike was all ready to pile into a cab and get settled at Bill's house, mostly so that he could call Pam and tell her how he was getting along. And to see how she was, of course, and if she had remembered to pay his medical insurance which in so many ways was beneficial to her as well as to Mike.

Bill seemed a little reticent about going home, but he took a deep breath, as if gathering his courage, and hailed a cab all the same. When Mike tried to open the door, the driver shouted at him and then—with some fanfare—pushed a button that popped open the doors automatically. After Mike and Bill had gotten inside, with their luggage and packages, the driver pushed another button and the door sprang shut, effectively locking them in for the duration of the ride. Mike didn't particularly like being sealed in that way, but he decided not to test the system. He was of the opinion that it was their country and they could operate it the way they wanted.

Mike never saw a driver take so many turns in his life and could have sworn they passed the department store two or three times. But he kept quiet about it. Maybe it was some kind of superstition—to go back to where you started a few times before really taking off. Or maybe it was the Japanese way of building up a head of steam for a long journey. Much to Mike's relief, they passed quite a few medical installations, each marked by a white cross. He had been worried about getting sick in a country as unusual as Japan. Bill explained that the little installations weren't really clinics at all, but brothels in which the girls dressed up as nurses and the customers got decked out in hospital gowns. Apparently, there was a great demand among the Japanese people for this type of operation, which was now franchised. But Bill told Mike not to worry since he knew some terrific dentists and foot doctors—in case Mike ran into any trouble.

The driver slowed down alongside a private home that was sandwiched between an apartment compound and what appeared to be a bustling little kimono shop. It was quite pleasant and countrylike, although the neighboring structures did seem to weigh in against it. Bill signaled the driver to stop, but after consulting his map, the independent fellow decided they were in the wrong place and kept going. It took quite a bit of shouting and explaining to convince the driver that they had indeed arrived at Bill's house. He may never have been convinced. They piled out of the car with Mike offering to pay the driver and Bill having none of it.

"No way," said Bill. "When you visit me, I pay. When I visit you, you pay."

Mike hadn't actually thought in terms of a reciprocal visit from Bill, but he was sure it would work out all right if it came to that. There was an extra room that could be fixed up in no time—and Pam would make him feel comfortable once she got used to the idea of having guests, which quite truthfully, she wasn't too crazy about. And that included her own folks. But any such visit was way off in the future and there was no point in worrying about it now.

MIKE MEETS BILL'S FAMILY AND THEIR STRANGE BOARDER

TO GET to the house, Bill and Mike walked through a lush and exquisitely tangled garden. They passed several rippling brooks and a bamboo waterfall. Plump and hardy carp leaped from the water as if to greet them.

"This is quite a spread you've got here," said Mike, trying to take it all in.

"Not really," said Bill. "It's only one-eighth of an acre."

Mike took a more careful look around and saw that the spacious feeling came from tilted hedges and a few artfully arranged mirrors.

"Why, it's just a little bit of a place," he thought to himself, comparing it to some of the roomy spreads in his neck

45

of the woods. But they sure knew what to do with it.

A mountain of newspapers and periodicals had accumulated on the veranda, almost as tall as Bill himself.

"Always happens when you take a trip," said Mike sympathetically.

"No, no," said Bill. "This is just two days' worth. We have a lot of subscriptions."

"Well," he said, wearily scooping up a bundle. "Might as well get started reading them."

A young fellow flew out of the front door and right up into Bill's arms. Apart from the glasses, he was the spitting image of old Bill himself, and Mike felt confident that this was Bill Atenabe, Jr. The boy wept tears of joy at seeing his father and Bill wept a flood as well. Mike was about to weigh in with some tears of his own when the youngster, still in his father's arms, whipped out a pad and pencil and began to scribble some notes. Bill did not reprimand him so much as to ask him what was up. Embarrassed, the boy mumbled something in his father's ear and then ran into the house.

"He had to finish up an essay," said Bill, by way of explanation.

"But you've been away for a month," said Mike.

"They work the boys very hard," said Bill.

"You'll catch up with him after school," said Mike.

"He goes to school after school," said Bill.

Before entering the house, Bill kicked off his shoes, Mike following his lead without missing a beat. It was the one custom he knew something about. Then they entered the house which was light and airy and spacious, although it was tough to tell exactly where the rooms were. The space kind of slipped and slid and refracted and Mike couldn't tell if there was too little of it, too much, or just enough. On the one hand, it was as open and pristine an environment as he had come across. Yet when he looked around, he saw that every conceivable space was crammed with what appeared to be thousands of household items, all neatly stacked and organized. Bill took Mike's things and amazingly found a compartment that seemed to fit them to a T, with not an inch to spare.

"It's as if you've been waiting for me," said Mike.

"Maybe we have," said Bill. It was the first cryptic remark he'd made since they'd begun their friendship.

Bill then showed Mike to his room which, so far as Mike could tell, was just an area with no definable boundaries. No question, there was enough space for Mike to get around in, but it just wasn't a *room* by his standards. Nonetheless, he leaned against a wall and did the best he could to relax and feel at home.

Anticipating Mike's thoughts, Bill arranged a long-distance call to the States. Next thing he knew, Mike was leaning against a mantlepiece, talking to his honey as if she were just around the corner.

Pam sounded a little stiff and secretarial and when Mike asked her about that she insisted that everything was tip-top and that she didn't know what he was talking about. He finally got her to admit that she had just started on a pizza and was watching her favorite daytime show, which she said she would happily turn off. Mike brought her up to date on his adventures in Japan, focusing on his friendship with Bill and the featherduster incident in the department store.

"So you're having a great time," said Pam.

"Oh yes," said Mike. "This was absolutely the right thing to do."

"I'm so-o-o-o happy for you, babe," said Pam.

"But don't you still love me," said Mike, pretty confident he knew the answer.

"Oh God," said Pam. "I love you so much I could scream."

"And don't take this wrong," she added, lowering her voice, "or think I'm putting any pressure on you, but I am very very HORNY."

"I am, too," said Mike, which, strictly speaking, was not one hundred percent true at that particular moment. How could it be when he wasn't really settled into his new environment.

"And I guarantee you we will make up for it the second I see you."

He didn't say when that would be and Pam was careful not to ask.

They exchanged more I-love-you's and then Pam said: "Just make sure those Japanese wenches don't see your legs and tush."

"Ah honey," said Mike, "they don't care about that." But he certainly liked being teased in that manner.

"The hell they don't," said Pam.

Through a large bay window, Mike saw Poppa Kobe get out of a cab, pursued by a young Japanese woman holding a clipboard and taking notes. Poppa Kobe seemed agitated which in turn got Mike upset. After all, he was Bill's dad. Perhaps a bit too briskly, he told Pam he had to get going, but that he would be in touch. Then he hung up the phone quickly and in the process knocked a small vase full of ashes off the mantlepiece. Bill came running over and tried to scoop up the ashes and pour them back into the vase. What Mike thought was a mantlepiece turned out to be a Shinto shrine. The ashes were those of a recently departed uncle, fortunately not one favored by the family but a relation all the same. It was required that his remains be kept in the shrine for a year before he got to return to the City of the Dead. The ashes could then be recalled for short visits from time to time, but only if someone felt an honest yen to be in touch with the fellow.

Mike got down on his knees beside Bill and went to work. All things considered, they did a pretty good job of getting the fellow's remains back in the vase before Poppa Kobe walked in.

Raising a fist, Poppa Kobe shouted at Bill, who tried to calm him down. Then Bill raced outside—once he understood what was bothering the old-timer. Mike followed his friend — and guess who had goofed again? Mike, after removing his shoes, had pointed them in a direction that indicated he would be staying with the Atenabe family for at least a couple of years. That was about as far from Mike's intentions as you could get. But there didn't seem to be any way to get this across to Poppa Kobe, who went grumbling off in another direction, with the slender young girl at his heels. She looked just like a walking flower, and was, no contest, the prettiest girl Mike had seen in Japan thus far. What made it strange was that she looked Japanese from head to toe. It was then that Mike became aware of a prejudice that he hadn't realized was part of his makeup: that Oriental women were attractive to him in direct proportion to how much they resembled American women. Well, that was something he would have to correct.

Mike thought the woman was some kind of personal geisha, but as it turned out, she was the highly trained brain-squeezer Bill had told him about. Connected to the prestigious Todai University, she had been hired by Poppa Kobe's company and assigned to "squeeze" the old-timer as he approached noodle-time, or compulsory retirement.

Bill explained that Poppa Kobe had been a brilliant innovator in his youth and had actually made some strides in the development of an ironic computer. The question, however, was whether the company wanted one. If they had, Uncle Kobe would have been kept on past the standard retirement age. But in a close vote, they had decided to push on without one, effectively sealing Poppa Kobe's doom. Still, before casting him adrift, they were determined to get everything he had, intellectually speaking. Hence, the lovely brain-squeezer.

"Is it an accident that she's gorgeous?" asked Mike.

"They have some dogs, too," said Bill.

"Well," said Mike. "No wonder he's cranky all the time."

"And your shoes put him over the top," said Bill, unhelpfully.

Bill then made what Mike felt was an excellent suggestion—that they both freshen up from their long exhausting trip with a nice hot bath. He led Mike to the family tub and took the lead in whipping off his clothes. Then he settled into the steaming water slowly, behind first, said "Ahhh" as his seat hit the water, and kicked out his legs, snapping open a newspaper. Mike had seen old Jewish guys do the same thing in a Turkish bath.

He took off his own clothes, did a skinny-dipping leap into the tub and then settled into a corner of his own. Mike asked Bill if the newspaper carried American sports news and could he, perhaps, find out how the Islanders were doing. Bill riffled through the newspaper, but for the life of him could not seem to find the sports section. Finally, he located it where the obituaries used to be. He said the Japanese newspapers kept switching sections around to keep up their readers' interest. And the Islanders had won three in a row.

Just for the hell of it, Mike picked up one of Bill's newspapers and started to scan it, although, of course, he couldn't make head or tail out of it. About the only thing that made sense to him was a picture of Joan Collins waving either hello or good-bye at the airport. Bill suggested it wouldn't be all that impossible to master the reading of a Japanese newspaper since all you had to do was learn one thousand ideograms and you were home free. Mike was a pretty fast learner so he said he would give it a try. In no time at all, he had mastered the signs for "curvature of the spine" and "peninsula." But he could see that it was going to be a long haul and suggested they hold off for the time being and just enjoy the nice relaxing tub. Pam had been after Mike, as a shower person, to try a tub just once. She was confident it would make him a changed person and she, of course, was capable of disappearing in one for whole sections of the day. So he decided to take this opportunity to see what all the fuss was about. But no sooner had the two friends gotten settled in than a great commotion was heard down the hall. Japan seemed to be that kind of country; it would go along in a peaceful manner and then you'd have a great commotion. Bill and Mike slipped into blue silk kimonos and padded down the hall to the main area of the house, where they found Poppa Kobe storming up and down in a full-out rage. Mike cringed back, wondering what on earth his latest goof could have been. But as it happened he was in the clear on this occasion. The target of Poppa Kobe's fulminations was the flower-like brain-squeezer from Todai, who had somehow gone over the line in her attempt to extract all of his wisdom.

The old man circled her, shaking his fist, first at the squeezer and then at the gods. The young woman's reaction was to lower her head and cry. Mike longed to put his arms around her, in a protective manner, of course, the way he might comfort a graceful animal that had been injured in a Japanese forest. This turned out not to be necessary. Storming out of the kitchen came a jolly and robust woman who could only be Momma Kobe, Bill's mom. She rapped Poppa Kobe over the head with a vegetable steamer, not really hard enough to hurt him, but as if to knock some sense into his head. Then she shoved him along the corridor, chanting:

> Poppa Dopey
> Poppa Dopey
> Shame on you
> Shame on you

And then she returned to comfort the weeping girl. Mike noticed that Poppa Kobe had gone off meekly, and although the scene had been high-spirited, it had been carried off with a certain affection.

After Momma Kobe had calmed the young girl down and seen her to a separate wing of the house, she turned her attentions to Mike, looking at him as if he were a wonderful hunk of roast beef. There was no formality about her. She just grabbed him and pinched his cheeks and told him he was certainly welcome in the Atenabe home. There was no question that Bill had said a few words about him to his mom. She was so jolly and good-natured and Mike was so exhilarated by his foreign adventures that he couldn't resist pulling her to him and dancing her around the room a few times. You wouldn't know it to look at him, but Mike was a pretty smooth dancer and even knew a few tap steps. He broke away from her for a moment and performed some of these. At first Momma Kobe was taken aback. Then she got shy. And finally, she entered into the spirit of it and tried some steps of her own. Mike admired her for being dead game, but felt that her squat and stocky build interfered with her performance. Also, she was working with a quirky kind of Far East rhythm that was foreign to him, to say the least. Maybe she was good—by those standards—and *he* was the klutz. But what the hell, he figured, nobody's trying to be professional around here. So he swept her off the ground, waltzed her around a few more times and finished off the dance with an old-fashioned forties dip. The lovely Todai squeezer appeared and didn't seem to know what to make of all this, so she decided to take a few notes. Mike gave Momma Kobe a kiss for being such a good sport, then looked up to see a woman even bigger and wider than her come waddling out of the kitchen, waving a ladle and bellowing something that obviously had to do with dinner. Momma Kobe put a finger over her lips as if to say "Shhhhh" and then shoved the protesting newcomer back into the kitchen. She kept shoving people around and getting away with it, no doubt because of her essential good nature.

"That's Lydia," said Bill, "our Korean maid, who comes in on Tuesdays and Thursdays."

Bill said that Lydia had been with the Atenabes for many years and, despite the fact that the Koreans generally were considered an underclass, she was accepted as part of the family. Lydia had been brought to Japan many years back on a death march; but she liked what she saw and decided to stick around. She had a son who was always being picked up for crimes he didn't commit; whenever this happened, the Atenabes intervened, assuring the police that Ken was not the murderer or rapist they were looking for. Which to the best of their knowledge he wasn't. And Lydia had rewarded their kindness by continuing to work for them at a time when skilled cooks and housekeepers were at a premium.

Japan had given Mike a tremendous appetite and as a

result, the hour before dinner was not an easy one for him to get through. Bill had left him to his own devices and he was hungry enough to go out to the garden and wolf down a few tangerines. If that's what the little orange balls were. He didn't feel he knew the Atenabes well enough to slip into the kitchen and grab off a little sushi appetizer. Nor did he feel relaxed and secure enough to fall out on the tatami mat that Bill had provided for him at the foot of the bay window. He still wasn't sure where his room began and where it ended and he wasn't the kind of fellow who could take a nap in some vaguely defined area. So he just leaned on the mantlepiece for awhile, making sure he didn't dump over the remains of any relatives. Mike noticed that the Atenabes owned a menorah, a crucifix and a couple of Buddhist statuettes. They certainly did have their flanks covered in the religion department.

He was wondering about this when Bill jogged into view at long last, slapped him on the back and said: "Soup's on, fella."

DINNER IS SERVED

BILL LED Mike into the dining area and said that dinner
was to consist of corn soup, glazed eggplant, bean cakes,
the obligatory steaming bowls of rice and dried fish eggs.
Mike felt it was interesting as hell, but not, quite frankly,
the kind of meal that you could wrap yourself around. Not
if you were an American. Nonetheless, he concealed his
disappointment and was quickly rewarded with a tower-
ing stack of wheatcakes, placed at his elbow and obviously
whipped up with him in mind by the beaming Momma
Kobe and her Korean cohort.

He offered them around, but only Poppa Kobe lacka-
daisically speared a few. The lovely Todai squeezer sat

decorously at his side, although Mike sensed that she wanted to get in there and do a little deprogramming. If only she could find the right moment. Momma Kobe peeked in on her from time to time and seemed to tolerate her as she would a foolish mistress.

Mike now got to meet Bill's wife, Helen, a tall and handsome woman who appeared to be older than her husband and gave off a slight whiff of the high-born. Her kimono was far and away the most expensive-looking one Mike had seen thus far in Japan. Bill seemed terribly proud of her, his face lighting up as he introduced her to Mike.

"She did the eggplant," said Bill. "Isn't it delicious?"

"It certainly is," said Mike, taking a few more bites than he was in the mood for.

Helen told Mike that she was in the language department at Todai and had recently completed a paper on the remarkable similarities between Japanese and Hungarian. Mike said he never would have guessed such a thing, and Helen, as if spurred on by his comment, recited a poem that she had written. She did it for the table in general but more specifically for Mike—or at least that's the impression he got.

> The snow falls
> and covers the landscape
> like a white blanket
> how pure it is
> marked only by a drop of blood
> from my lover's soft breast

Mike assumed this was haiku, although he seemed to recall it needed a few more beats to qualify as such. Or a few less. It was a little spare for his taste, but that was probably the whole idea of it—to see how spare you could get. In any case, he said he thought it was just fine. Helen blushed and Bill, beaming at her once again, said: "You should hear it in Hungarian."

Eating began once again, with Mike trying his best to use good manners. He speared particles of rice that fell from his plate and licked off any food that remained on his chopsticks. Poppa Kobe groaned each time he did that, and of course, Mike found out later that chopstick-licking is one of the worst gaffes you can come up with at a Japanese dinner table.

Everyone sat in the duck-walking position, weight solidly back on the heels, and Mike felt grateful that his legs were in good shape. Restoring houses tended to keep them that way. Otherwise he would have been screaming in agony before he got past the first course. As a result of the odd seating arrangement, Mike kept getting unsolicited glimpses of Helen Atenabe's panties. Which he was not that anxious to get. No disrespect to her, but this was Bill's wife. Even setting that aside, he was in no mood to see anyone's distinguished panties during his first meal in Japan. If he *had* been anxious to see some, he would vastly have preferred to look at those of the Todai brain-squeezer—although why he was even *thinking* about panties was beyond him. Eight thousand miles away from home and Pam trusting him to do the right thing. If the meal had been just a little more fortifying he was confident that he would not have been focused on panties.

To avoid further embarrassment, Mike turned his attention to the tall shambler of a fellow on his right. And a fellow he was all right, although Mike wasn't quite sure the first time he looked at him. He wore white makeup and kept his hair rolled up in a chignon with a turquoise comb stuck through it. The fellow said his name was Juro and that he was an actor with a Kabuki-style theater group who boarded with the Atenabes. The performers were required to play both male and female roles so that Juro had to be ready to go either way at a moment's notice.

Mike found Juro a pleasing dinner companion with a gentle romantic style. Halfway along in his dinner, the actor whipped a *samisen* out of his kimono and began plucking melancholy chords on it, at the same time reciting verses which he explained dated back to the Edo period. Helen Atenabe sniffed a bit when he began them, but Juro continued right along, after giving her a disdainful look. The verses dealt with love affairs between sixteenth-century noblemen and brothel girls, all of the liaisons hopeless and culminating in joint suicides. As he played, Juro struck arrogant poses which he said were favored by young lords as they waited for their women in brothel anterooms. The spirit of his performance was quite romantic, causing Momma Kobe to squat beside her husband and hold his hand. The young Todai woman leaned forward and trembled as if shaken by the wind. The tenderness of the moment even drew Lydia from the kitchen. Mike himself got caught up in Juro's gentle presentation and sensed he was experiencing a side of Japan that was revealed to few westerners. And it was only his first day in the country.

But then the spell was broken by a great din outside the house, causing Juro to hit an imprecise note and the other diners to freeze in place.

AN UNWELCOME VISIT—AND BILL'S SAD EXPLANATION

A ROWDY group of several dozen young men wearing T-shirts and bandanas shouted and banged drums and seemed to be summoning someone from the household. Bill glanced outside and then hung his head in shame. Clenching his fists, Poppa Kobe threw out some guttural sounds but made no attempt to silence the mob. Helen Atenabe left the room. Mike was about to get to his feet— someone had to do *something,* he felt—when the tall, skinny-legged Juro broke a sake warmer and walked outside with the stride of a Samurai to confront the mob. Soon the noise died down and the group left, starting up their harassing chant when they were well away from the house and passing the property of some neighbors. Juro returned to his seat and continued to pluck chords on his *samisen*, but with no accompanying verses. Red-faced, close to tears, Bill ran out of the house. Mike started to follow his friend, but Juro put a hand on his shoulder and cautioned him not to do so.

Mike listened to Juro a while longer and after what he considered to be a discreet interval, said *"Itte mairimasu,"* excusing himself. He had a feeling the colloquialism would impress Juro, but the actor, who was lost in feudal romance, paid no attention to it.

Mike went into the kitchen to thank Lydia for the dinner, but the beefy Korean seemed to have taken off, leaving a sinkful of dirty dishes. If the rioters had set out to disrupt the harmony of the Atenabe household, they had certainly succeeded.

Mike thought he might as well help in the clean-up, but he couldn't seem to figure out the right commands for the dishwasher, which was voice-activated. So he wound up rinsing off the rice bowls by hand and stacking them neatly in the pantry. He figured it was the least he could do to repay the Atenabes for their hospitality. Then he made his way to the main living area where Poppa Kobe, the squeezer, and what appeared to be a group of neighbors were gathered around a TV set, watching a movie. It was about a wonderful mother who is great to her children, but winds up being turned out of the house all the same and pelted by rowdies. Everyone seemed to be crazy about it; they alternately wept and howled with laughter. Everyone, that is, except Momma Kobe. Off in a corner, she watched a TV monitor with a different ending, one in which the mother is welcomed back by the family.

Mike had trouble getting involved in either version and

slipped off to try to find his room, or at least his area. There was no point in being coy about it. That first day in Japan had been an exhausting one and he was anxious to hit the sack. Tentatively, he slid back a screen and saw immediately that he had made a mistake. Stretched out on a mat was Bill Atenabe, Jr., poring over a sheaf of Cheryl Tiegs glossies with a high-powered magnifier. Mike had wondered why the youngster hadn't eaten dinner with the family and assumed, no doubt along with the other Atenabes, that Bill Jr. couldn't spare the time from his studies. He certainly wasn't going to spill the beans, but it did make him wonder how many other Japanese youngsters, having perhaps cracked under exam pressure, were secretly poring over pictures of top models.

After quietly sliding back the screen, Mike was intercepted in the hallway by his friend Bill who put a finger to his lips and led him outside to the garden. A half moon and some stars seemed to be tacked on to the sky. Mike followed his friend along a pebbled pathway and through a small crawlspace that led to a bamboo shed. Bill seemed to be using it as a kind of clubhouse.

There, Bill lit some candles and produced a pair of ceremonial swords which he waved above his head.

"These are Nyudo weapons," said Bill. "They were molded in the Kamakura period and forged in incredibly pure steel, although frankly they could use a good sharpening.

"Mike," he said, dejectedly, "they're dull as butter knives. And I was going to demonstrate some Samurai moves, but frankly, I'm not in the mood."

Mike was sympathetic and said he could understand full well why someone might not want to demonstrate Samurai moves after a rough day.

"Thanks, Mike," said Bill, setting aside the swords. "Would you like some tea? To prepare it properly would take eight hours, but I'm willing to do it for you."

"I would just as soon pass," said Mike.

Bill seemed relieved. He reached into a refrigerator for a carton of beers and popped open a couple.

"I brought you in here to talk about my rife," said Bill.

It was the first time he had heard his friend lapse into pidgin English and Mike concluded it was the sensitivity of the subject that brought it on.

"Maybe it's her work," said Bill. "The second she proved there was a link-up between Japanese and Hungarian, she started to draw away from me. I'm scared, Mike. As of late, she's reduced me down to oral sex."

Mike said he was sorry to hear that, although frankly he knew of lots of fellows who could get through very nicely on such a diet. He saw no need to point out that even Pam—one of the most giving and compassionate creatures to walk the earth as far as he was concerned— had cut back his allotment in that department as soon as they began to live together.

Still, he told his friend to hang in there and things were bound to change.

"I don't think so," said Bill.

"Look out there," he continued, gesturing off in the moonlight. "The crickets are chirping, the dog is howling and I can hear the sigh of the cypress trees. Not only that, but there's a high wind from the North and we're in the 223rd day of the Year of the Rat."

"That may very well be," said Mike. "But it probably doesn't add up to a hill of beans."

Bill bared his teeth and reached for one of the swords, but then he tossed it aside.

"I forget," said Bill, sheepishly. "You're an old cutup."

"No, I'm not," said Mike, refusing to give ground. "Despite all those signs, a fella can still be in great shape."

"Not a Japanese fella," said Bill.

"Suit yourself," said Mike. "And incidentally, what was that ruckus outside the house?"

Bill said that he had lost a great deal of money on high-school basketball games in the States, and that the Yakuza, with whom he had placed his bets, had set out to shame him in front of his neighbors.

"That's another reason my rife is down on me," said Bill, with another embarrassing lapse into pidgin.

Mike said that he was surprised to see that Juro was able to get them to back off.   ▶

"He seems like such a frail person."

"Yes," said Bill, "but they heard his belly."

He explained that the Japanese communicated powerful emotions through that part of the anatomy.

"Obviously," he continued, "they didn't hear mine."

Mike told Bill not to get down on himself, and that everyone made a stupid mistake once in a while, although he personally didn't understand risking great sums on sporting events.

"Still," he said, "if it's money, maybe I can help out."

He said he had laid aside some funds in triple-tax-exempt municipals which, frankly, he wasn't anxious to tamper with.

"But if you need it, Bill, it's yours."

"I would hate to take it from you," said Bill, "but I may have to."

"Then just holler," Mike said uneasily.

Then he poked his friend in the belly with the tip of the short sword and said: "Now let's get some sack time."

"Why, you hamburger," said Bill, taking a swipe at Mike's legs with the long one.

Mike got in a couple of quick ones and Bill threw back his head and let fly some yodeling cries that seemed to be designed to signal the commencement of battle. Then he went into a bandy-legged fighting crouch and they were off, leaping and dodging, hacking and thwacking at each other in the moonlight. It was a miracle they didn't wake the neighborhood, or worse, that someone didn't get an eye yanked out or a leg sawed off. They instinctively took just enough off the thrusts to render them playful rather than destructive, although a miscalculation would have been costly. Finally, the two friends fell against the house, winded and exhausted, Mike satisfied in the knowledge that, for the moment, he had been able to distract Bill from his misery.

"Thanks, Mike," said Bill, fighting for breath. "I know you were doing a little psychological work on my head, but I appreciate it."

"No sweat," said Mike. "And now, can we PLEASE get some sack time."

"You got it," said Bill and led Mike off to his area which had been cordoned off by sliding screens and looked exactly like a real room. In addition, Mike's clothing had been set up neatly on a dressing tray and someone had thoughtfully placed a silver pitcher beside his mat.

The two friends said goodnight, and then Mike, after a quick wash-up, got into a thin sleeping kimono and stretched out for the night, his long legs extending well past the lower edge of the tatami mat. He'd had quite a day for himself and longed to share the details with Pam— although, in truth, it generally took her half an hour to settle in for one of his stories. First she had to wander around for a while and get her coffee and even cook up some fresh popcorn. By then, he had usually lost his enthusiasm. Still, there was no denying he was crazy about her. He was determined to focus on Pam and keep thinking about her until he fell asleep. And he would have, too, if some loose doggerel hadn't started to fly around in his head and to repeat itself maddeningly:

> She's a kamikaze mother
> kami-kaze mother
> in love
> with her
> su-i-cidal son

MIKE VISITS BILL'S COMPANY AND GETS ONE OF HIS HARE-BRAINED IDEAS

MIKE MADE his way to the kitchen the next morning and found Bill slumped over the table, reading *Asahi Shimbun* and sipping some black tea.

"Mornings are rough for me," said Bill. "I thought I might as well warn you."

"You're not that great at night, either," said Mike, slipping Bill a friendly needle.

But it went right past Bill, who insisted he improved as the day went along.

Lydia put a plate of prawns in front of Mike, which was not his idea of a breakfast, although he had to admit they were great-looking prawns. She also shoved a stack of magazines in front of Bill.

"Oh my God," said Bill. "The monthlies are here. How will I ever get through them?"

"Who said you had to?" said Mike, taking a bite of a prawn and lusting for a buttered bagel.

"Are you kidding," said Bill. "What if I missed something?"

"Such as what?"

"Say they found the bones of a thousand-year-old man in Kamakura. I'd be the only one in Tokyo who didn't know about it."

"Wouldn't the dailies cover it?"

"Not necessarily."

"Then *skim* the damned things," said Mike, rolling up a monthly and smacking his friend on the head with it.

"*Skim* it," said Bill, derisively. "That's easy for *you* to say, you Bronx bomber." He rolled up a monthly of his own and the two friends would have gone at it again if Juro, who was sitting in a corner, hadn't shushed them down. He was playing chess with a computer.

"Sorry, Juro," said Bill, going back to his newspaper.

Billy Atenabe, Jr. came flying down the corridor shouting: "I'm late for school. Oh my God, I'm late." And then he bolted through the door and was gone.

"He sure does take his education seriously," said Mike, not letting on about the Cheryl Tiegs glossies.

"We all do," said Bill. "It's gotten us where we are today."

After he had eaten the last prawn he could handle, Mike asked Bill what the agenda was for the day.

"I have to see Mr. Ito, the company director, and get deprogrammed. Care to come along?"

"Of course," said Mike. "You didn't think I was here to see the temples, did you?"

"What's wrong with our temples, Mike?"

"Nothing, for God's sake. You sure are touchy."

"I guess I am, Mike. I'm Japanese."

"And I'm American."

"That's the whole point," said Bill. "You defeated us in the war and we're a little cranky about it."

"I can see that, Bill. Would you like me to leave?"

"Of course not, Mike. Somebody had to lose. It's just too bad it was us."

"All right, that did it," said Mike, getting up from the table. He didn't know where he was going, but he was determined to go somewhere. Maybe he would give one of those mail-slot hotels a shot after all.

"Come on, Mike," said Bill, stopping him. "Who's being touchy now? I love you, you big Yankee bean soup."

Mike felt that the bean-soup analogy was a shade off, but he was moved all the same.

"Tell me about Pam," said Bill, as they drove off to the train station in Bill's car.

"She's the nicest, most caring person I've ever known," said Mike.

"That's all very well," said Bill, with an unbecoming leer. "But you know, *tell* me about her."

"She can laugh with her eyes," said Mike.

"That's impossible," said Bill.

"Not in Pam's case."

"All right," said Bill. "I'll let you have that one."

"You won't let me have anything," said Mike, getting his back up. "She laughs with her goddamned eyes."

"I'd like to see that some day."

"Maybe you will," said Mike, who was getting more and more irritated by the minute. Still, he went on about Pam. "She's real pretty and she's got this great body except that she won't flaunt it."

"Why is that, Mike?" Bill seemed to ask the question with genuine curiosity.

"Because she doesn't want to," said Mike. "For Christ's sake, you guys *invented* modesty."

"And a sorry day it was," said Bill, who in many ways was the moodiest fellow Mike had ever encountered. He was all over the road. Was this representative of the Japanese character, Mike wondered. Had he come to a nation of moody guys? Or was Bill a special case?

These were Mike's thoughts as they joined a throng of early-morning commuters at the train station.

"I've heard about this," said Mike. "They say a couple of attendants come along just before the doors close and shove in the passengers who can't squeeze in by themselves."

"That's not true," said Bill, airily. "It was some bad publicity we got."

But sure enough, when the train stopped, two attendants pushed and shoved the overflow of passengers aboard before the doors slid shut.

"A famous first," said Bill, dismissively.

"And I just don't understand these crowds," he continued, as he and Mike struggled to find a little space for themselves. "It must be a convention. Otherwise we'd have the whole train to ourselves."

Mike found himself pinned up against a distinguished-looking elderly gentleman who was reading a comic book that featured drawings of shackled campfire girls. He held it closer so Mike could have a look, but Mike declined, muttering something about it being a little early in the day for that sort of thing. Off in the corner stood a younger-looking executive-type with an old woman on his back. She was cronelike and seemed to be eating nuts.

"What's the deal on that fellow?" asked Mike.

"That's his mom," said Bill. "He can't bear to be separated from her so he's taking her to work. She has arthritis."

"What will he do with her when he gets there?" asked Mike.

"Set her down in the lounge and resume his managerial functions. There are some other moms for her to be with. At the end of the day, she'll hop back on her son and they'll take the long journey home. He's got quite a commute."

"Very strange."

"Not really," said Bill. "We're much more of a matriarchal society than people realize. And did it ever occur to you that maybe you seem strange to us?"

"Touché, Bill," said Mike.

"I didn't mean to give you a zinger, but sometimes you ask for it, big fella."

"I understand, Bill," said Mike.

The guard at the gate looked at Mike suspiciously, but after checking Bill's security pass, he waved them both on.

"What's in a name, eh, Mike?" said Bill. "Plenty. The Atenabes go all the way back to the Tokugawa period. We got to wear three swords while the peasants didn't get to wear any. And we had so many hectares of land we didn't know what to do with them."

"Got any left?" asked Mike.

"A few," said Bill guardedly.

A platoon of uniformed workers came marching by in military formation, chanting what Mike took to be the company song and waving their arms in military precision. Just for the hell of it, Mike fell in with them and began to shout out a few marching commands of his own. This threw off the group's rhythm and it seemed to lose its direction, a few of its members drifting into a cafeteria.

"For God's sake," said Bill. "What are you doing? I have to face these men every day."

"Calm down, Bill," said Mike. "I was just trying to loosen them up a little. Everything's so regimented around here."

"Well, cool it," said Bill, who certainly had picked up a lot of stateside lingo during his recent tour. "And besides, if you think *we're* regimented, wait till you see our Fifth Generation boys. This is spit."

The teams on the assembly line seemed every bit as brisk and efficient as they were cracked up to be, except for one group of fellows who were casually sunning themselves against the factory walls.

"What's the deal on those fellows?" asked Mike.

"Those are our Lazy Boys, Mike."

"How come they're not working?"

"They don't feel like it," said Bill, who seemed surprised that Mike would ask such a question.

"Then how come they're not thrown out?" said Mike, finding himself, surprisingly, on the side of the company.

"Why do that?" said Bill. "Why shame them? Do you want to send them home to their families with an empty rice bowl?"

"*I* don't," said Mike, "but doesn't it knock hell out of your production output?"

"Are you kidding?" said Bill, with a touch of smugness. "Care to see some stats?"

Mike had to admit that Bill had him there—he was well aware of Japan's astonishing emergence as an industrial giant. And he was becoming more and more fascinated by the long lines of wiry little guys on the line. He wondered what it would be like to get in there with them and slap a few components together. To be part of a team for a change instead of being such an independent guy. The idea took hold of him and it was all he could do to keep from yanking one of them out of there and taking his place.

Instead of just muscling his way in, he asked his friend if it would be possible for a fellow like himself to tie on with such an outfit for a while.

Bill shook his head and said it was a tall order. Even if such a thing were possible, it would take six months on the average to get a response from the company. But then he pointed to a muscular little man who was on his knees polishing machinery and said: "You're in luck, Mike. That's Mr. Ito. We may have a chance. Even though my father is being forcibly retired, the Atenabe name still goes a long way around here."

Mike couldn't believe that the unassuming fellow was in charge of the entire company.

"He is, Mike, all two hundred thousand of us."

"Then why is he polishing machinery?" asked Mike, an obvious question if ever there was one.

"Most people think he's trying to set an example," said Bill. "But that's not it at all. He just likes to polish things. It gives him a good overall feeling. I'll see what I can do with him."

Mr. Ito seemed pleased to see Bill. The two had a spirited conversation during which Bill pointed to Mike a few times. Mr. Ito gave him a couple of friendly waves.

But when Bill came back, he said it was no go.

"I couldn't budge him, Mike. He just doesn't want you on the line. If you're interested in sales and promotion, he'll take it up with his colleagues."

"It's the line or nothing," said Mike. "I can't explain it but I've just got to get in there with those guys. Maybe it's because I've worked alone for so long. Rick doesn't count. He's so goddamned spooky he hardly even talks to you."

Now that he thought about it, Mike realized that after he finished up working alone, he'd go back home to the woods and be alone with Pam. As exciting a person as she was, she was also so goddamned self-sufficient she hardly needed him.

"I've practically got to get an audience with you," he would joke and she would say, "You've got me here all the time," and go back into one of her novels about the English gentry. Mike didn't have any family, although he and Pam had talked casually about starting one. Yet neither one seemed to want to be the first to broach the subject in a serious manner. He and Pam had moved deep into the woods, after agreeing that the city "tore you up." But apart from isolation, there really wasn't that much out there in the woods. Was it possible that's why he had come to Japan—to get some people to hang out with?

"I'll keep after Mr. Ito," said Bill, "but it's a long shot."

"How come he smiled at me in such an encouraging way?" asked Mike, following his friend down a flight of stairs.

"That's pretty standard," said Bill. "But if you recall, he also fanned his face. That should have been the tip-off."

Bill led Mike along a dark tunnel.

"I still can't believe that little fellow is in charge of such a giant operation."

"He is, Mike," said Bill, "and easy on the height jokes."

"Is there any chance he'll change his mind?" asked Mike, as they stepped through some revolving doors and entered a latrine area.

"Once he makes a decision, that's pretty much it," said Bill. "That's because he hardly ever makes one. And also, he's probably a little afraid you'll take his job."

"But that's absurd."

"Not to Ito. You're a big strong fellow and strange things happen. It's a feeling he has and feelings are most important here in Japan."

"Well, what are *we?*" said Mike. "A bunch of robots?"

"We don't believe in robots," said Bill. "We're just trying to fake other countries into building them."

"Lovely," said Mike.

"Competitive," said Bill.

After they'd used the urinals, Bill showed Mike some graffiti on the back wall of the lavatory.

One said: *Our section leader has several flaws.*

Another, furtively scrawled, said: *Work, work, work. Surely there are other important things in life.*

"What do you think of that," asked Bill, lowering his voice to a whisper.

"It's a little mild."

"You really think so?" said Bill, taken aback. "I thought it was rather daring."

"Not where I come from."

"Now look, Mike," said Bill, with an edge to his voice. "Those fellows risked a lot putting that graffiti up there. If they were found out, they'd be dead in Japanese industry. Don't go making fun of them."

"I'm not, Bill. I just thought the messages could have had a little more bite to them."

"You and your pipe dreams," said Bill.

Back on the main floor, Mike noticed some of the workers tossing little pieces of paper into what looked like a wishing well.

"That's a suggestion box," explained Bill. "It's very popular because the company uses almost every suggestion they get."

"I've got one for them," said Mike. "Move the men's room closer to the workers. We had to walk a mile to get to it."

"They won't use that one, Mike. It's been tried. If they followed your plan they'd have calm workers. The company likes to keep them a little edgy."

"Sounds cruel."

"There's a cruel streak in our culture, Mike, as evidenced by the writings of Tanizakai Junichiro. He once wrote a story about a fellow who lived in a hotel lobby chair."

"That's not cruel. It's erotic."

"Are you kidding, Mike? All those fat ladies sitting on the guy?"

"I'll bet *you'd* like to slip into one of those chairs, you horny Nip."

Bill made a serious face. "I understand the spirit in which you made that remark, and I am not offended. But lighten up all the same. Remember, I've got troubles at home, Mike. I'm sad."

Mike decided to switch gears before his friend got any more morose.

"And I'm starved," he said. "What are the chances for some chow?"

"Excellent," said Bill, leading him out to the factory yard where the two purchased little buckets of noodles from a vendor.

"You've been a great pal and a perfect host," said Mike, "but the truth is, I haven't had one thing to eat that I can actually wrap myself around."

"Tonight's the night," said Bill. "We'll get ourselves some mittu and sarad."

It took a few beats for Mike to realize his friend was talking about meat and salad.

"Just out of curiosity," he asked. "How do you say a thing like that in Japanese."

"I don't know," said Bill. "But it's an excellent question. I'll ask Poppa Kobe. He might be old enough to remember."

A whistle blew and hundreds of workers came streaming out of the plant, taking up positions on one side of a hastily constructed barricade. A long line of executives in black suits filed out of an administrative building and took up their own positions opposite the workers. At a signal, the two sides then glared at each other in a hostile manner. Mr. Ito came running out of the plant in shirtsleeves and coveralls and at first seemed puzzled, lining up beside the workers. But then, realizing he might have committed a gaffe, he rolled down his sleeves, slipped into a blue suit jacket that was handed to him by one of the executives and hopped over to the management side.

"Looks like we've got a strike on our hands," said Bill.

The two factions hurled epithets at one another for awhile, but then settled into a silence. This was followed by a pained, mewling sound from both workers and management, as the two sides struggled to resist reaching out to one another. Finally, both factions could bear it no longer and went leaping across the barricade, flinging their arms around each other in an outpouring of tears and emotion. Then, arm in arm, the workers and management people marched back into the plant singing the company song. One worker attempted to hoist Mr. Ito atop his shoulders, but the company director swatted down at him until the overenthusiastic fellow released him.

"Damned thing couldn't have taken more than twenty minutes," said Mike.

"It's one of the longest we've ever had," said Bill.

"I don't see why they even bothered."

"It's expected of us, Mike. As you can see, everyone is crazy about the company. But we don't want other countries to think less of us, so we have a strike now and then."

"Weren't there any issues?" asked Mike.

"The workers wanted Mr. Ito to have a bigger office. They felt shamed by his small cubicle. But when he gave in on that point, the strike fell apart."

Bill said he had to go get debriefed by Mr. Ito and suggested that Mike might want to visit a nearby park and take in a fertility festival.

"I think you'd enjoy it, Mike. They pass out herring eggs to ensure lots of babies."

Mike said he'd prefer to pass but wondered if Bill would mind setting up another call to Pam.

"I'd be happy to," said Bill, leading Mike over to the administration building. "You really love her, don't you, Mike?"

"I don't know how I can stand being away from her."

"You could always bring her over," said Bill.

"I thought of that, but at this precise moment, it would throw off my rhythm."

In Mr. Ito's outer office, Bill turned Mike over to a squadron of thin little women in kimonos who took off his shoes, loosened his collar and dusted off the phone. Then they served him a variety of beancakes and put through a call to Pam, fanning him as he spoke.

"How's it goin'?" she asked.

"Just fine, babe. I've had a lot of interesting experiences."

"Such as?"

"It's hard to single one out. There have been a whole cascade of them."

"I'm glad, hon. Any idea of when you'll be back?"

"I just got here, hon. I don't actually have my teeth in the country yet. If I left now, it would blow the whole thing."

"I don't want you to do that, babe. Mort and I miss you, but we don't want you to come home till you've finished what you set out to do."

"Truthfully, hon, I'm not sure what that is."

"It doesn't matter. I know you. You'll find out when you do it."

"How the hell did I get so lucky?" said Mike.

"About what?"

"Landing you."

"I'm the lucky one, hon."

"The hell you are. But listen, take care of yourself. This isn't going to take forever."

"I know, babe. And you be careful, too."

"I'm insane about you."

"I'm insane about you, too."

When Bill came out of Mr. Ito's office, he found Mike in tears.

"Everything all right, Mike?"

"Yes. That's why I'm crying. I can't get over how wonderful that girl is."

"I envy you," said Bill. "That and your height."

"It'll happen to you, Bill."

"No, it won't. It's not in the cards."

"It wasn't in the cards for me either, Bill. And yet it happened. Pam just sneaked up on me."

"She's not sneaky, is she?"

"No," said Mike with a chuckle. "She's just the opposite."

He asked Bill how he'd made out on his debriefing session.

"Ito wasn't interested in my findings. He felt my entire trip to the United States was a waste of time."

"You didn't lose your job, did you?"

"Oh no," said Bill. "They're stuck with me till retirement. Then I can be thrown out, just like my father. In the meanwhile, they'll just have to find something else for me to do. But Ito told me to keep after you about a job in sales and promotion."

"I'm not interested in any of that," said Mike.

"It's the elevator division he's concerned about. They can't seem to get rid of their cars. Ito thinks a big strong American fella like yourself might make a difference."

"Out of the question," said Mike. "I'd walk right out on the assembly line in a second—I'm dying to, for that matter—but it's the line or nothing."

"You're stubborn, Mike. Ito senses that. You may have a little Japanese in you."

"Wouldn't that be something," said Mike.

STRANGE DOINGS AT BILL'S CLUB.
MIKE MEETS A WOMAN OF THE PLEASURE QUARTER.

JUST AS Bill had promised, they ate a fine western-style dinner at a restaurant that seated no more than a dozen people. The furnishings were so spare and the decor so classically simple that Mike assumed it catered to a limited and exclusive clientele. But Bill said quite the contrary— the owner had been trying to add a few tables and get some more people in there, but a dozen was about all they had been able to attract. One problem was that the owner didn't really like the smell of Westerners. Mike looked over at the fellow who had seated them and sure enough, he kept one shoulder hunched and crinkled his nose.

"Why doesn't he go into another business?" asked Mike.

"It's all the poor guy knows," said Bill.

During the dinner, Bill kept disappearing behind a curtain and emerging with a white speck beneath his nose. Mike wondered if his friend hadn't succumbed to drug addiction and decided to ask him about it as Bill called for the check.

"It's no shame," said Mike. "It's actually spread through just about every layer of society. And I'll hang right in there with you while you try to kick it."

Bill said he was clean as a whistle in the drug department, but that like virtually every Japanese, he was subject to rice rushes. Even though the restaurant catered to Western tastes, a giant vat of hot rice was kept in the kitchen so that Japanese customers could slip back and take tokes of it.

"All that rice intake piles up over the years," said Bill, patting his middle with satisfaction, "giving us the low, sloping belly that's so admired and envied throughout the world."

Mike had his doubts as to whether the type of belly described by Bill was really all that sought after by non-Japanese, but decided not to challenge his friend on the issue.

On the way to his club, Bill asked the cab driver to stop in front of a two-story wooden house on a narrow lane.

"I just want to check in with my astrologer," said Bill, "and I promise not to be long."

Ten minutes later, Mike saw his friend go flying off the roof of the house, arms and legs flailing wildly, and land in a ditch.

He rushed to Bill's side and asked him what on God's earth had happened.

"It was a test, Mike. If I had landed lightly on my feet, then everything would have worked out fine for me in the next month.

"But I guess I've got some rough weather up ahead," said Bill, who could barely get to a standing position.

Mike suggested that Bill see a doctor, but his friend said he preferred to get cleaned up at the club and let nature take its course. Mike was inclined to dismiss the astrologer's theory as hogwash, but as the two friends drove along in the cab he began to think that there might be something to it.

"I guess if you were in a peaceful, Zen-like state, your muscles would have been relaxed and you probably *would* have landed without hurting yourself."

"Don't complicate things," said Bill. "Just pray that I haven't broken any bones."

The owner of the club was a hearty fellow who greeted Bill and Mike with a booming *"Hirasha maise,"* just about breaking Mike's eardrums in the process. Following right behind him was a lovely fresh-faced woman in a kimono who welcomed Bill with a combination of East-West styles, first prostrating herself before him, palms downward, then leaping to her feet and giggling over Bill's tattered condition. The fact that she teased him and didn't fall all over him with pity led Mike to believe that she really liked his friend. The owner escorted Bill and Mike to a modest-looking bar where each bottle was displayed in its own richly cushioned case, bearing what appeared to be a family seal. Bill asked if anyone had taken so much as a sip of his bottle during his absence, whereupon the owner shook his head vigorously as if to indicate it was worth his life to prevent such a stain on Bill's honor. Then Bill poured a couple of whiskeys, took a sip of his and shook his head with satisfaction.

"What a pleasure to drink your own whiskey," he said.

"If anyone had sneaked some, there would be trouble between our families, possibly dragging on for years."

"That seems a bit extreme," said Mike. For all of its fancy presentation, it was, he noticed, just popular-brand scotch in the medium-price range.

"Not to us," said his friend.

Bill laid the bottle back gently in its case and led Mike over to a cabaret-style table, where the woman, whose name was Suzue, washed Bill's wounds with warm, scented cloths and scolded him for not writing her a letter when he was in the States.

"I was worried about you," she said. "And I *missed* you, you big gorilla.

"Those legs," she said, pinching Bill at the knees and making a growling sound. "Those fat and beautiful bowed legs. Don't think I didn't miss them, too."

"Put on my cassette," said Bill, ignoring her affectionate remarks. At this command, Suzue assumed an obedient style, bowing deferentially and then running with quick steps to what appeared to be a control room.

"She's wonderful," said Mike. "And she really loves you."

"Are you crazy," said Bill. "She's a woman of the pleasure quarter."

"What does that mean?"

"It means that she's insincere."

"So what," said Mike. "If what I saw is the result, what difference does it make?"

"Wow," said Bill, shaking his head, "you sure are naive about night women. Here," he said, clapping his hands, "let me show you."

A second woman, smaller and leaner than Suzue, came running out with light little steps.

Bill gave her a command, at which point she hopped

on Mike's lap, put her arms around him and said: "How are you doing, big boy. What strong muscles you have. I'll bet you are some hot lover. Care to squeeze a little titty?"

"My case rests," said Bill, obviously pleased with himself.

"That wasn't the same thing," said Mike, setting the woman aside and trying to hold down his temper.

"Can't you see the difference, you stupid eggroll?"

He realized the "eggroll" reference was imprecise and possibly a tad on the offensive side, but he decided to let it stand.

"Mike," said Bill, soothingly. "I know you're my friend, but you really don't understand our world. Take my word for it. Both girls are artificial."

Now it was Mike's turn to feel glum. Here was Bill with love staring him right in the face and the poor bastard didn't even know it. Mike missed Pam terribly and felt like chucking the whole visit right there and going back to her. What a dumb country and what a dumb friend he had. The only thing that stopped him from pulling out right then and there was Pam herself, who unquestionably missed him but who'd be let down if he returned before he found out why he went there in the first place. So Mike decided to hang in for a while. The more brash of the two girls, whose name was Nanae, sat at his feet and stroked his knees and he had to admit to a slight curiosity about that titty invitation of hers, as crass and insincere as it no doubt was.

Some executive types in black suits began to arrive, stripping down to their underwear and garters and taking seats in the cabaret section. Mike couldn't help but comment on this odd behavior, which Bill said was part of the club style. He suggested that before the evening ended, he and

Mike should get into *their* underwear so as not to show disrespect to the membership.

"You *have* been wearing underwear, haven't you?" asked Bill.

"Of course," said Mike, who was surprised rather than offended.

"I just wanted to make sure," said Bill. "We hadn't discussed it, but it's a tremendous insult to your host if you don't."

When their private bottles had been brought by clusters of night girls, the executives relaxed a bit and grunted at each other. Mike hadn't realized there were so many different types of grunts and Bill confirmed that the varieties were virtually uncountable. Mike tried a few of his own and the executives looked over, having obviously spotted his as counterfeit.

Some background music came on and Bill got to his feet and sang a couple of choruses of "I've Got You Under My Skin" in a thin but pleasant voice. One of the executives snapped his fingers, calling for *his* background music; when it came on, he did an up-tempo version of "That Old Black Magic" and was hissed into silence.

"He's lucky he didn't get thrown out," said Bill, reacting to the fellow's disagreeable singing style.

"On his fat ass," said the night girl named Nanae who was perched at Mike's feet.

"Leave your wife," she whispered to Mike, her lips wet and her nostrils quivering. "Run away with Nanae."

This definitely struck Mike as being insincere, although he had to admit it was not entirely without appeal.

A fellow dressed in an oversized and outdated tuxedo entered the club and began to move deliberately from one table to the next, stopping for a moment to take a quick swig from Bill's family bottle, then pushing on and sitting at a table of his own.

"I guess that means war," said Mike, getting to his feet and rolling up his sleeves.

"Not exactly," said Bill. He eased Mike back into his seat and explained that the tuxedoed fellow was a top Yakuza, the man responsible for sending the crowd of rowdies to harass Bill at his home.

"I owe Shigeko a hundred grand," said Bill. "So I guess he's entitled to a few sips."

The fellow lit a cigarette and signaled to Bill, who—to Mike's way of thinking—ran over a little too obediently.

When Bill returned, he said that Shigeko had asked all about Mike. Upon learning that he was an American, the gambler had asked to have a word with him.

Mike said he wasn't too crazy about the idea—but he would do it since it seemed to be important to his friend Bill.

With some stiffness, he approached the table of Shigeko, who asked Mike how Jacqueline Onassis was doing. The top Yakuza looked straight ahead and did not meet the American's eyes.

"All right, as far as I know," said Mike.

"She's my favorite individual in the whole world," said Shigeko. "You agree?"

Mike said he felt she had some fine qualities, although he could not honestly say she was his absolute favorite person in the world.

Shigeko thought that over, curling some smoke through his nose, and seemed to decide it was an acceptable answer.

"When you see her," he said, "tell her that if anyone harms her, or if she needs anything, to let Shigeko know."

Mike said that they didn't run in the same circles, but if he happened to bump into her, he would let the former First Lady know.

"And there'll be something in it for you," said Shigeko, tapping his breast pocket and making it clear that he was a student of forties gangster films.

By the time Mike returned to Bill's table, Shigeko was already sauntering toward the exit, stopping only to pinch Suzue's buttocks in a conspicuous manner.

"He's a mutt," said Mike.

"That may be," said Bill sadly. "But I owe that mutt a lot of money. Can you imagine! Losing a hundred grand on American high-school basketball games."

"How could you do that, Bill? Nobody knows who's going to win those things."

"I thought I did," said Bill.

"Any way you can pay him off?" asked Mike.

"I could sell my part of the family property, but then I'd be the first Atenabe in history without any hectares."

"Do it, Bill," said Suzue. "I'll stand by you. And if all is lost, you can live with me on my farm in Kyoto."

Bill shook his head and laughed at what he perceived to be her insincerity.

They listened to music and drank a lot of sake.

"I just don't feel this stuff," said Mike, when it appeared to be closing time. It seemed to him he had drunk a gallon of it.

"It's tricky," said Bill. "Watch the way it affects you when you stand up."

"It still hasn't hit me," said Mike, who had gotten to his feet easily. To show what good shape he was in, he leaped up and clicked his heels a few times.

Bill said he would take Mike's word for it. But it was

important that they join the departing executives in stag-
gering out the door.

"Club style?" asked Mike.

"Exactly."

Mike did the best job he could of pretending to reel
toward the exit. Suzue was waiting there and asked Bill if
she could meet him on the outside someday.

"I want to so badly," she said, clutching his arm.

Bill ignored her and signed his tab.

"You mean to tell me she makes that same pitch to every
guy who comes in here?" said Mike.

Bill admitted there was no evidence of her ever having
asked another club member to meet her on the outside,
but that it was beside the point.

"Once and for all, she's from the pleasure quarter, Mike,
and as such, her words are meaningless."

"I still think you're making a big mistake," said Mike.

"Your friend is right," said Nanae, pulling Mike aside.
"*I'm* the sincere one. No man has ever thrilled me more
than you have, Yank. And believe me, I've run into plenty.
Meet me on the outside, Mike, and I'll show you pleasures
you've never dreamed of."

At this point, Mike was fairly certain that Nanae was
insincere. But he had to admit he was far from offended
by her style.

AN ODD MEANS OF CONVEYANCE

THE TWO friends stumbled out into the night, arms around each other, singing and howling at the moon and giving off the impression that they were every bit as wasted as the other club members. The more Mike pretended, the more rambunctious he got. Finally, Bill had to quiet him down for fear they'd rouse the neighborhood.

They took a train back to Bill's house and got off one stop before their destination. Two stocky fellows ran forward carrying a boxlike litter on two poles. It was big enough to accommodate two men. Bill said it was a *kago*, used for transport in ancient times.

"It's a novelty, Mike. I ordered it up because I thought you might enjoy it."

The two men got inside and once they had settled back in their seats, the husky fellows lifted the enclosure and trotted off with them.

In the darkness, Mike could hear the two litter bearers grunting away and said he felt a little funny about them.

"I know you meant well," he said, "and that you no doubt paid them a lot. But I wonder if they should be doing this kind of work—in this day and age."

"Actually, I didn't pay them, Mike. They asked *me* for the work. They're trying to build up their legs for the Olympics."

The darkness and the swaying motion of the compartment was soothing after the activity at the club.

"All right," said Bill, out of nowhere, "what if I did leave my wife and go to live with Suzue in Kyoto and we had a child together and I was happy for the rest of my days. It would all be an illusion."

"We've got fellows in our country who say it's all an illusion anyway."

"Yours is a strange country," said Bill. "I never could get a handle on it."

Juro seemed to be the only member of the Atenabe household who was still awake. The tall slender actor was listening to a Fats Waller composition on a cassette player, accompanying the jazz great with his *samisen*. After greeting Bill and Mike, he challenged the two *kago* bearers to a foot race. They willingly accepted and the trio went flying off in the moonlight.

"It seems an odd time to go racing," said Mike.

"Not for Juro," said Bill. "He practices the Mie style of acting which requires freezing the body in contorted positions for as long as three-quarters of an hour to drive home a particular emotion. It's rough on a fellow Juro's age, with his poor circulation and skinny legs. So he leaps at every chance he gets to keep his blood moving.

"He'll surprise those husky guys with how well he does in the short distance—although they'll overtake him if they don't lose heart."

The two sat down at the kitchen table and Mike popped one of the rice balls that Lydia had set aside as a late-night snack. She had also provided slices of fresh carp along with a note saying that she would have done much more, but her son was in trouble with the police again.

"So what do you think of our Japan so far?" asked Bill, popping a rice ball of his own.

"I notice I'm paying a lot more attention to small things," said Mike. "The striping on this carp, for example. The way the room screens whistle in the wind. The nape of a girl's neck."

"The nape of a girl's neck is no small matter," said Bill. "Men have left home for less. But generally speaking, you're on your way to understanding us. We're a nation of precise detail."

Then he looked off toward a distant mountain and groaned. "I just wish to *God* we had a big picture."

Mike, who had finally gotten the hang of the time differential, called Pam before he went to bed and told her about the night at the Club and how he had gotten involved in his friend Bill's unsettled domestic life.

"Don't tell me you've taken on another case," she groaned, in reference to a handful of fellows he saw on rare occasions. He considered them fascinating and she saw them as deadbeats. They were named Whaler and Snuff and "Busy" Finkelstein.

"I think I have," said Mike. "But the main thing is I don't know how much longer I can stand being away from you. Why don't you hop a plane and come on over?"

"You're a sweetbomb for saying that, Mike, but don't they have a lot of crowds over there? You know how I am about crowds, the way I freak. You don't even get to go to the movies because of me, you poor thing."

Mike said Japan wasn't as crowded as she imagined, although he had to confess that you did run into a human wave from time to time.

"So maybe it's best that I hurry up and get my business done so I can be back where I belong."

"You don't have to *hurry* hurry," said Pam. "That's not what I mean. I just miss your bones."

"And I miss yours, honey. This is not going to take forever. I'm practically walking in the door."

MIKE GETS HIS WISH.
HE HOOKS UP WITH IRV MIYAKAWA AND THE ENGAGING SEASONALS.

THE NEXT morning, Bill said that Poppa Kobe had intervened on Mike's behalf and gotten him a job on the assembly line after all.

Mike was delighted but couldn't help wondering how the old-timer had been able to pull it off.

"Isn't he on his way out?" asked Mike. "And why would he do a thing like that for me?"

"It's true he's being forcibly retired," said Bill, "but he's still an Atenabe, which counts for a lot. They don't want him to go away completely disgruntled. He did the favor for you because he knows you've seen me through some rough spots. Also, he's heard that you've been cleaning up the kitchen late at night—without being asked. So he's heavily in your debt, Mike, although God knows, he doesn't want to be."

"Tell him it's even-steven, after the factory job."

"It doesn't work that way," said Bill. "Debts take a long time to discharge. Right this very minute he's probably bitterly planning his next favor to you. So please don't do anything else nice for him or it'll go on forever."

"I'll cool out the good behavior," said Mike. "And boy, is this job exciting."

"I know," said Bill, who was all awash in a fresh new wave of publications that had poured in that morning. "Now will you please let me try to make a *dent* in the biweeklies."

Bill Jr. came down shortly thereafter and said he'd like to forget about his upcoming college entry exam, quit school altogether and become a show business agent.

"Very funny," said Bill. "Now run off to school before I kick your tush."

"I'm serious, dad," said the youngster.

"So am I," said Bill, chasing him out the door.

"What if he really meant it?" asked Mike. He thought of the night he'd discovered the boy poring over glossy photographs of Cheryl Tiegs. What if the boy's interest had been strictly professional?

"The whole communications field is exploding," Mike continued. "Would it be a tragedy?"

"Worse," said Bill. "It would be the end of the Atenabe family."

After breakfast, Bill and Mike joined Momma and Poppa Kobe at the police box where the elderly couple were trying to get Lydia's son out of custody.

When they arrived, an officer was explaining to Bill's parents why they were holding him. Lydia was in tears and the boy was being guarded carefully by a deputy. He was a handsome young lad, although in truth, he seemed a little shifty-eyed, at least to Mike's eyes. Then again, who wouldn't be after constantly being tapped on the shoulder by the police?

"There have been a rash of robberies in the area," said the officer. "Since he's the only Korean we could find, we had no choice but to hold him."

"Look for some more," said Poppa Kobe, unhelpfully. Momma Kobe shushed her husband down and took over.

"So he's Korean," she said. "What does that prove?"

"That he's responsible," said the officer. "Who else would commit such crimes."

"Did you ever consider that it might be one of our own Japanese?" suggested Momma Kobe.

"Madam," said the officer, dismissively. "I'm a busy man. Don't waste my time with these absurdities."

"Take him away," he ordered the deputy.

"He's a good boy," said Lydia, flinging herself at the officer's feet. "He'd be in the army if you had one."

"We can't be expected to have an army just so the Koreans can have something to do."

"Poppa Kobe," said Momma Kobe, poking her husband with an umbrella. "Wake up and guarantee the boy some work."

With a broad wink to his wife, Poppa Kobe said he would see to it that the boy was put on typhoon patrol.

"All right," said the officer, pushing forward some documents for the Atenabes to sign. "But make sure there are no more crimes around here."

"Make sure your wife wears a decent kimono," said the

feisty Momma Kobe, rising up to her full though modest height.

"I give her the finest," said the officer, who seemed shaken.

"I said your *wife*," said Momma Kobe. "Not your woman of the pleasure quarter."

With that, she led the Atenabes and the Koreans out into the street. There, Bill explained that for all practical purposes, Poppa Kobe had arranged for the young man to be put in the army.

"Let's face it, Mike, there just aren't that many typhoons in Japan. We call our soldiers, "typhoon workers" so as not to upset other countries. We've probably got the most powerful army in the world."

"Would you use it again?"

"Don't mess with us, Mike. We're not just a bunch of little cassette guys."

"Still," said Mike, moving away from the uncomfortable subject, "it's a shame they have to keep hounding that youngster."

"Not really," said Bill. "Ken probably did commit some of those robberies. We just help him out because of his mother. It's impossible to get good help around here."

Mike made an attempt to thank Poppa Kobe for getting him a job on the assembly line, but the old-timer drove off with his wife and the Koreans before he could do so.

"It's just as well," said Bill, starting up his Saab. "He feels bad enough being in your debt as it is. Why rub it in?"

In Mr. Ito's outer office, Bill coached Mike on how to deal with the company director at this stage.

"Make sure to say you're ashamed of yourself," said Bill.

"But I'm not," said Mike. "Why should I be?"

"It's not important," said Bill. "It's just a way to get off on the right foot."

At the meeting that followed, Mike took Bill's advice and said he was ashamed of himself, after which Mr. Ito said he was even more ashamed of himself than Mike.

"I don't know about that," said Mike, looking at Bill for further instructions.

Bill jumped in and said that Mr. Ito no doubt was more ashamed of himself than Mike but that Mike would do his damnedest to catch up. That seemed to placate Mr. Ito, who led Bill and Mike in some company fight chants and then sent them off to join their unit.

Bill said he would be working closely with Mike, which would give *him* a chance to learn the assembly line as well.

"It's company policy to switch people around to different divisions so they can learn the whole operation. And of course, they don't know quite what to do with me."

Bill told Mike that they had, indeed, been assigned to elevator cars—the weakest division in the company.

"They're way behind on their schedule—and the cars they do turn out tend to stall between floors. It doesn't really matter, since they're sent to Singapore, but Ito has some important buyers coming in from the West Coast. He'd like nothing more than to get the quality level up— and sell them a few. Ever since Ito pulled himself out of the wartime rubble in Yokohama, it's always been his dream to have his elevator cars running in downtown L.A."

"If nothing else, I'm a competitive sonofabitch," said Mike. "I can hardly wait to get out there on the line and see what I can do."

"Ito spotted that," said Bill.

* * *

At the assembly line, Mike met the members of his immediate unit which was to consist of Bill and himself, a stocky, good-natured supervisor named Irv Miyakawa and half a dozen dejected looking "seasonals" from Yokohama. Irv explained that, in addition, Ito would be filling in from time to time although he'd been having trouble getting a good pair of safety shoes.

Using a numbered diagram, Irv described Mike's function on the line, which was to receive the top of an elevator from Bill, secure a dozen fastenings, then walk across the line, fit the piece to the body of the elevator and slide it along to the seasonals for final assembly.

"If you can do that in a minute and eight seconds," said the friendly supervisor, "we're off and running."

"I'll bring it in under a minute," said Mike.

"I wouldn't be too sure of that, Mike," said Irv, "although those long arms of yours should help. You're replacing a fellow who could barely reach the top of the car and, of course, that really killed us."

Irv distributed a guidebook of instructions on how to ward off muggers in the Tokyo subway—and then led Mike aside to a nearby bench.

"How are you getting along at home?" he asked, putting an arm around Mike's shoulders. "It's my job to help out on personal problems. And it's all right, Mike, you can just let it pour out. You'll feel better. Hell, don't we all have troubles from time to time? Unload your guts to me, big fella."

Mike said that he appreciated Irv's concern, but that to the best of his knowledge, he and Pam were getting along just fine.

"Well," said Irv, getting to his feet with a sigh. "I can see this is going to be a tough one. All right, we'll let it sit for now. But remember, when you're ready to spill your pippick, you can trust Irv Miyakawa."

Mike and Bill spent the rest of the morning in a dry run, working without the actual elevator car tops, while the seasonals, who'd already been trained, looked on glumly.

When it was time for lunch, Mike and Bill asked Irv if he would like to take his noodles with them at a nearby park. Irv thanked them, but said he had already planned to have some eel soup at his bench and study the new manuals. The seasonals took their noontime break at a nearby Temple for the Unmourned Dead.

"Won't that be a little depressing for them?" asked Mike, as he and Bill wolfed down their noodles.

"Not really," said Bill. "It's the only place they can relax. They have a rough life, Mike. They were really happy back on the farm. Now they sleep in a cold dormitory and go to bed with blow-up dolls. If you stand nearby, you can hear them crying themselves to sleep. I wouldn't be a bit surprised if one of them was responsible for some of that inflammatory graffiti I showed you."

Mike felt that he had made his feelings clear as to the mildness of the latrine scribblings and decided to let the remark go by.

"No wonder production is so low in this unit," he said.

"It sure doesn't help," said Bill.

"What's the story on Irv?"

"He'll never show it, but the failure of this unit is really killing him. He came over from a crack semiconductor chip team and he'd always been a winner until he got into elevator cars. Now he's so upset that he doesn't even stay out all night and drink. He goes right home to his wife and family, quietly accepting the abuse it brings him in the neighborhood."

"I'd sure like to help the guy," said Mike.

"He knows that, Mike. *He* knows it, *I* know it and the *seasonals* know it. The problem is, they don't care."

When Bill and Mike took their places on the line after lunch, it quickly became apparent that improving production and quality wasn't going to be any cakewalk. With all the encouragement in the world from Irv Miyakawa, Mike was hard pressed to get his own time down below three minutes. One of the problems seemed to be that Bill didn't seem cut out for work on the line. His mind tended to wander so that a lot of Mike's time was wasted in waiting for his friend's "hand-off." Then too, every now and then a seasonal got homesick and burst into tears, which would completely throw off the rhythm of the unit. Irv would have to pull the emergency switch and stop the line until the poor fellow got himself together, all of which ate up valuable time. In spite of this, the seasonals were a surprisingly nimble lot once they got going and Mike saw that they were the beginnings of a fine team. By the end of the day, however, he could barely move his arms and legs; it was with some relief that he heard the closing whistle blow. Bill and Mike changed into their street clothes, waved good-bye to the seasonals and asked Irv if he would care to join them for a drink. Once again, Irv declined, saying he was going to stick around and see if he could push out another half a car before he went home.

"Need any help?" asked Mike, although in truth he wasn't at all sure he had anything left in the tank.

"That's all right," said Irv, reaching for a power screwdriver. "You fellows go off and have a good time."

"Now I feel a little guilty," said Mike, as they walked to the parking lot.

"You shouldn't," said Bill. "The company is his life. It was mine, too, but I've gotten more freewheeling since my month in Manhattan."

SICK IN A STRANGE LAND—MIKE'S NIGHTMARE COME TRUE

BILL REMEMBERED that he had to see someone off at the airport and wondered if Mike would care to come along. After that, the plan was to have dinner at Bill's club and start drinking so that they would be assured of rolling in at four or five in the morning. Thus, Bill's stature among his fellow workers and in the neighborhood would be maintained.

Mike said that of course he'd be happy to join Bill, although by the time they reached the airport his upper body was fairly numb and he had broken out in a fever.

"How long have you known this fellow?" asked Mike

as they joined a group of well-wishers who were seeing off a middle-aged man in a dark suit.

"I just spoke to him once at a cocktail party," said Bill, waving to the fellow as he strolled toward the aircraft.

"Then how come you're seeing him off?" asked Mike.

"Because it's fun," said Bill. "It's one of the most Japanese things you can do, to see a countryman off on a trip. There's another fellow leaving from Tokyo Station in an hour. I shook hands with him once. He'll only be away for a weekend, but I'd like to say good-bye to him anyway. We can make it if we hurry."

"I think I'm going to have to pass on that," said Mike who could barely walk and whose teeth were beginning to chatter.

"You just don't know what a good time is," said Bill, who seemed disappointed. But once he realized how awful Mike looked, he helped his friend back to the car and drove him to the Atenabe household.

"That's the last thing I wanted to happen," said Mike, as Bill helped him through the garden. "Getting sick in a foreign country."

"There's no better place to get sick than Japan," said Bill. "How would you like to trade places with me—having to face my rife in broad daylight."

Try as he might, Bill simply could not pronounce the delicate word in the correct manner.

Much to Bill's relief, Lydia said that Helen Atenabe had been called off to the university to do an emergency translation of some Hungarian literary criticism. Momma and Poppa Kobe were attending a benefit for a friend named James "Happy" Mirimoto who had flown twenty kamikaze missions during the war, failing on each occasion to blow up either himself or his target. For some reason this had made him a bit of a celebrity. Bill Jr. was closeted with a professor whose function it was to pick him up after a full day of school and then coach him from six o'clock in the evening until two in the morning, thus assuring his acceptance into a fine university.

Bill moved Mike's things into a more spacious, four-mat room and helped him change into a light kimono. Then he eased Mike down on the most comfortable tatami mat in the household and gave him a small indoor kite to play with while he went off to call for help. Mike made a few attempts to set it aloft, but was so enfeebled that he soon gave up in despair.

Soon afterward, a van pulled up carrying a team of doctors and medical technicians, all in white uniforms. Silently they filed into the house and began to uncrate their equipment. In a flash, Mike found himself hooked up to a complex series of scanning machines that appeared to be monitoring his every bodily function. Simultaneously, a word processor typed out a report; within half an hour, Mike was handed a bound volume containing the team's findings.

After Bill had thanked the medical personnel on Mike's behalf, they bowed politely, folded up their equipment and slipped quietly out of the house.

Mike was too weak to deal with the report and asked Bill to review it for him.

"This is your complete medical history," said Bill after a quick riffle. "It also contains a diagnosis of your current condition—extreme exhaustion and aggravated muscle fatigue—plus a projection of problems you can expect to run into in the future. Further up ahead, you might keep an eye on your prostate."

"Did they prescribe any medication?" asked Mike.

"They don't do that," said Bill. "They're diagnosticians. You've put your finger on one of the weaknesses in our system. It would take around ten days before I could get anyone over here to actually treat you.

"My suggestion is that you take a couple of aspirins and try to get some sleep."

Mike followed his friend's advice and had a dream about Prague, another city he had never before visited. In it, he was hitting all the Prague spots and wasn't in the least bit sick. When he awakened, Irv Miyakawa and three of the seasonals were squatting beside his mat, watching him anxiously. He realized he must have been asleep for twenty-four hours.

"Oh my God," said Mike, trying to sit up. "I've let you guys down."

"Put that out of your mind for the moment," said Irv, as the three seasonals began to blush. "The important thing is for you to get better."

Mike asked what the group had done in his absence.

"Mr. Ito filled in and actually handled himself quite well," said Irv. "His height is against him, of course, but as you know he's quite spry and has a good attitude. He had other duties, of course, but he said he'd help out part-time until you recover. And the seasonals have volunteered to do double shifts."

The three men lowered their eyes and pawed at the floor.

"I'll be frank with you," said Irv. "The L.A. buyers will be along in about ten days, so we're a little pressed for time. Schwartz heads their team and we've never been able to sell him so much as a matchstick. If we don't get some excellent cars out, he'll be in touch with Sony before we know what hit us."

"I'll be in tomorrow for sure," said Mike.

"Not unless you're fit as a fiddle. The company is all-important, of course, but the workers' health is taken into account, too," said Irv, somewhat confusingly.

Bill came in with some fresh beancakes and said that the seasonals had brought Mike a box of fireflies but were too shy to say anything about it. As the three part-time workers looked away, Bill said they wanted it known that the insects were a present from *all* the seasonals, not just the ones in the room. The others were just too down in the mouth to visit.

"And here's a bonus," said Irv, handing him an envelope.

"But I've only put in one day of work," said Mike.

"That's exactly when the company does it," said Bill. "When you're down and out."

For a second, Mike thought he had an insight into why Japan had become such an industrial giant.

"And it comes out of my pocket," said Irv with some pride. "Not only that, but I only make a few dollars more than you do.

"And the seasonals make even less," he said. The three fellows grinned, almost as if in approval of their impoverished state.

"Well then, I can't possibly take this money," said Mike.

Irv bared some stumplike teeth and began to hiss at Mike, who reconsidered and tucked the envelope into a sleeve of his kimono.

"Thanks, Irv," said Mike. "I'll find a way to repay this."

"I sure could use the help," said Irv. Then he asked Bill and the seasonals if he could have a private word with Mike.

"What's the story?" he asked, when they were alone. "Are you sure this isn't all in your head?"

"Absolutely," said Mike, although he noticed that he hadn't been in any hurry to tell Pam he'd taken a job in Japan.

"Okay," said Irv, with a sigh. "But I promise, you'll feel better if you spit it up."

To get Irv off his back, Mike said that Pam sometimes annoyed him by not cleaning out the vegetable compartment of the refrigerator.

"Not that I'd mind cleaning it out myself," said Mike. "I'd do it in a second. But she says she'll do it and then she doesn't."

"Anything else?"

"I bought her some black silk Frederick's of Hollywood underwear and she hasn't worn it yet."

"And yet just two minutes ago, I sat in this very room and heard you say that everything was fine."

"It is," Mike insisted. "She'll wear it. She's just waiting for the right occasion."

"Sure," Irv mumbled. "And Korea's our best friend."

"Well, how do you feel now," Irv asked aloud. "A little better?"

"Sort of," said Mike.

"Good," said Irv, getting to his feet. "Now you just keep spitting this stuff up and we'll have you back on your feet in no time."

"I still think it was all that work I did the first day."

"Sure, fella," said Irv. "That's what they all say."

After he left, Mike wondered if there was anything to what Irv had said. Was he really sick because of the vegetable compartment and Pam's underwear? Maybe he should have said something about Pam taking up the entire clothing hamper. At the moment all he knew was that he was anxious to get back to the line as soon as possible, but that he still could barely move his arms and legs. This forced him to remain stretched out on his mat for several days more.

Among those looking in on him was the unemployed actor, Juro, who helped Mike pass the time by teaching him the ancient game of Go. When Juro first called on him, he carried his stones and board in a magnificent lacquered box, one that Mike calculated must have been a hundred years old. Mike praised the box lavishly, causing Juro to growl and hiss at him. Without realizing it, he had put the actor in the position of having to offer the box to Mike, as a matter of honor. Obviously Juro didn't really want to part with the box and was filled with shame. Mike was able to convince him that he didn't covet the set; and under no circumstances would he accept it as a gift. As a matter of fact, he insisted on giving *Juro* a gift and would pick one out as soon as he recovered. Somewhat placated, Juro patiently taught Mike the game, complimenting him on the speed with which he learned the rules and on the aggressiveness of his play.

After several nights, Juro suggested they place a small bet on the outcome of the game—to keep up interest. Mike, of course, readily agreed and before long had lost his bonus along with thousands in markers, which of course, he felt honor-bound to pay, especially in a country like Japan.

Throughout the day, Lydia brought him varieties of hot tea; he almost screamed out for a cup of coffee. The Korean housekeeper said that her son was coming along nicely in typhoon patrol and hadn't been arrested for some time. Additionally, he had become romantically involved with a member of Japan's despised *Burakumin* group. He and the lovely Undesirable planned to get married as soon as they had saved some money.

Mike couldn't help wondering why the struggling young

Korean would want to get involved with a total outcast. Clearly, the union of a Korean and a *Burakumin* spelled round-the-clock trouble. Still, it was their lives they were fooling around with. And who knew, perhaps love would triumph.

"Ken asked me," said Lydia, "if you'd care to buy his collection of fuck films."

At first, Mike was stunned by the casual tone of her proposal. Were the Japanese right, after all, in considering the Koreans a coarse and inferior people? But then he realized that sex had always come unaccompanied by shame in both countries, at least until the West had put its two cents in. Mike declined the porno flick offer but said he might be interested in a cassette of Sugar Ray Robinson's greatest bouts.

"Is he the one who—pound for pound—was your best fighter?" asked Lydia.

"Yes," said Mike, marveling at the breadth of her knowledge of American sports.

"I think my son has it," said Lydia.

Though no doctor was available to treat Mike, Bill was able to round up a neighbor who felt for illness through Mike's kimono, using the heel of one hand and marking the trouble spots for easy recognition. Then, obviously working on poor information, he whipped out some squares of putty. Before Mike could utter a word of protest, he had been fitted up for a death mask. When Bill came home from work and heard about this, he agreed that the neighbor had far exceeded his authority. He rang up the fellow and assured him that Mike had an excellent chance of recovery and there was no need to go ahead with the mask. Fortunately, the neighbor had not yet put it in the oven and was able to salvage most of his materials.

* * *

Late one night, Mike dutifully watched his fireflies, although, in truth, he couldn't really get too swept up by their activities. And then he called Pam and said the reason he hadn't been in touch was that he'd been ill and didn't want to frighten her.

"But it's all right, hon," he said. "I've turned the corner and I'm feeling much better."

"You got sick in *Japan?*" she said. "Oh Mike, how *could* you?"

"I didn't come over here to get sick," he said. "I was helping out some guys..."

"What kind of guys?" she asked.

"On an assembly line...I probably went at it too hard."

"Oh, Mike, I'm so disappointed."

"Well, don't scold me. I'm not fully recovered yet."

"I'm not. I was just hoping you'd call with some *good* news."

"I did. The good news is that I love you and I'm practically walking in the door."

"I love you, too," she said, a little petulant. "I just don't understand going all the way to Japan to get sick."

The next morning, Momma Kobe propped him up and shaved him and told him he looked like a doll. When she finished, Mike asked for a mirror so he could see for himself. Bill helped set one up for him and Mike noticed that his eyebrows had been trimmed and appeared to have been raised a bit so that he looked a little Japanese. He said he wasn't sure he wanted to go that way, but Momma Kobe told him to relax, they would grow back in no time. And in the meanwhile, the girls would be falling all over him.

When the color had returned to Mike's cheeks, Bill announced that Poppa Kobe, still in Mike's debt and hating every moment of it, had invited the two of them on his annual Peeper's Tour. It was sponsored by the old-timer's World War II Association, a group of fellows who had refused to surrender to the Americans for a long time after the war—and still weren't too happy that they finally had.

Mike felt he had a pretty good idea of what kind of tour it was but decided to check with Bill all the same.

"You peep on girls," said his friend.

"Any old girls?" asked Mike.

"It's all arranged. You'll see."

Mike said he appreciated the offer but that he felt a little uneasy about that kind of thing, especially in the company of a whole group of strangers. But when Bill said his refusal would be a blow of crushing magnitude to the old man, Mike agreed to go along.

"WELCOME BACK, MIKE."

THE FOLLOWING day, Mike returned to the line with renewed vigor, and in the week that followed, got his personal time down to the point that it was on a par with that of the short fellow he had replaced.

The seasonals showed their delight at having Mike back by showering him with fistfuls of rice which they quickly picked up so as not to be wasteful. Irv Miyakawa suggested they celebrate the team's progress—and Mike's return—with a lunch in the rain. Mike wondered if it was to appease a rain god, but Irv said no, it was just that the Japanese loved to be out in the rain.

On the day of the lunch, it really poured, and the seasonals had the time of their lives, prancing about and doing somersaults. It was the happiest that Mike had ever seen them. Apparently they came from a rainy part of Japan and felt right at home.

Only Bill Atenabe seemed a little down in the mouth. He said he had been offered an assistant coaching slot with the Hiroshima Carp baseball team. It was a lifelong dream, but he would probably have to decline. Mike said it was ridiculous, that he obviously wasn't cut out for the assembly line, but Bill said a change of career was out of the question.

"It would finish off Poppa Kobe," he said. "Even though he's being forcibly retired at the height of his powers, he wants me to stay on and rise with the company so that I can follow in his footsteps and be thrown out, too."

"And then there's my rife," said Bill, making the pidgin slip that seemed automatic each time he talked about his domestic life. "She'd never allow me to do something I had my heart set on."

"Maybe she'd admire you more if you stood up to her," said Mike.

"Helen?" said Bill. "She'd divorce me on the spot."

Mike joined Irv Miyakawa, who was trying to eat his noodles and at the same time protect them from the downpour. Irv said he was pleased that the team was getting out so many cars but that Quality Control had reported they would unquestionably fail in emergencies and trap the occupants on the higher floors. Once again, it was of no great consequence if a car were to break down and endanger its passengers on a high floor in Singapore. But the cars would never get past Schwartz and his team of L.A. buyers who were to arrive imminently. Mike said he thought he knew what Irv meant. Despite the improvement in production speed, the unit still had a certain rigidity to its performance, which probably found its way into the finished product. Mike said he wasn't sure what the wrinkle was but that he was willing to kill himself to find out.

"No, you won't," said Irv, taking a bite of his soaked noodles. "You'll leave us, just when the going gets rough."

"What makes you say that?" asked Mike, a little hurt.

"Because they all do," said Irv, the rain splashing on his thick glasses.

"What do you mean, 'all'?"

"Anyone who comes to work here who's not Japanese. They all pull out in the clutch. That's why Japan is so solidly Japanese. It isn't that we love each other so much. It's just that other people come here, tease us, and then disappear. So we have no choice but to fall back on each other. You will, too, Mike."

"The hell I will."

"You'll see."

"Now listen, Irv," said Mike, getting his back up. "I'll *never* leave."

And then he wondered if he really meant it.

POPPA KOBE'S EXTRAORDINARY PEEPER'S TOUR

AT DAWN, the members of Poppa Kobe's Peeping Tour assembled at the Atenabe house for a substantial breakfast and then silently filed into a van—as if they were preparing for a military operation. Behind the wheel of the vehicle was James "Happy" Mirimoto, the kamikaze pilot who had failed to execute dozens of suicide missions and yet somehow emerged as a national cult hero. Bill told Mike that in the last stages of war, when his hopelessness as a kamikaze pilot had been established, "Happy" had served as a scout for Poppa Kobe's unit, the two of them holding out on a grassy atoll for several years after the armistice.

119

"Those two guys really grew to love each other," said Bill.

Indeed, Poppa Kobe sat at "Happy" Mirimoto's side, while the others, including Bill and Mike, wearing baseball caps and flowered shirts, squatted in the main body of the van. Binoculars had been distributed by Poppa Kobe and each man assigned a small slit in the otherwise windowless van. Despite the absence of much light, the mood was festive, with many a cry of *"Banzai"* as the group set out on the first leg of its operation.

Gradually, however, the peepers quieted down; there was a certain tension in the air as "Happy" Mirimoto pulled the van into the parking lot of a fast-food emporium. At first, Mike thought they might be stopping for a bite to eat, which seemed odd since Lydia had prepared an enormous breakfast for them only a short time before. But then Poppa Kobe put a finger to his lips and signaled for each tour member to take up a position at his slit; Mike saw they were after different game.

In the corner of the lot, a pretty young girl in blue jeans tried vainly to start her pick-up truck. After several attempts ended in frustration, she walked to the rear of the truck, put her back against the vehicle, hoisted her legs against a railing and strained with all her energy to get the pick-up to move. For some reason, this struck Mike as one of the most erotic episodes he had ever witnessed. It was all he could do to keep from clawing at himself in frustration.

"Am I crazy," he asked Bill, "or is that one of the hottest things I've ever seen?"

"Quiet," said Bill, eyes glued to his own slit. "We'll analyze it later."

The girl spent about ten minutes straining to move the

pick-up truck. Finally, her blue jeans and T-shirt streaked with perspiration, she threw up her hands and sat on the railing, arms folded, as if waiting for help. Each of the tour members let out a satisfied *"Hai"* as "Happy" Mirimoto started up the van and once again took off along the highway.

"Why did that get me so excited?" asked Mike, returning to the theme.

"I'm not sure," said Bill. "You'll have to ask Poppa Kobe. He's the one who planned the tour."

Mike looked over at Bill's father with new respect. Somehow he hadn't seen him as being quite that sophisticated. But it fit in, actually, with his having allegedly designed the world's first ironic computer for the Ito Company. He was certainly a complex individual, which was obviously why the company wanted to drain off every bit of his knowledge before sending him off to open a noodle shop.

"Happy" Mirimoto next pulled the van alongside the curb of a somewhat crowded shopping mall. After checking his watch, Poppa Kobe once again signaled the tour members to go to their slits. Soon, a young woman appeared, smartly dressed in the western style. She was fresh and fair-skinned and struggled under the load of a shopping bag, filled to overflowing with freshly purchased items. Suddenly, her heel appeared to catch at an obstruction in the sidewalk. The load became too much for her and the bag fell out of her hands, scattering its contents over the sidewalk. She knelt, a little hopelessly, and at that moment, Mike once again felt a surge of eroticism, equal to the one he had experienced at the pick-up truck. And he'd thought for a while that he had left that side of him behind. And what was it really that had stimulated him— a girl kneeling, her skirt barely above her knees, flailing about to regain her purchases. Why was it having such an effect on him? No question she was graceful. Several times she brushed her long ink-black hair back past her ears. He longed to run out and help her but stayed glued to his slit in the dark. The other fellows on the tour held their positions as well, hardly drawing a breath.

"He's done it again," said Mike to Bill, who squinted with intensity beside him.

"Dad always comes through," said Bill, using the familiar phrase for the first time.

Before taking a break for lunch, the tour group peered through a dormitory window and saw a young coed in bra and panties, chewing bubble gum and lazily doing her homework—a tableau that seemed a bit studied. They also lined up outside a bank and looked in on an attractive young clerk, mechanically counting out cash and occasionally reaching back to straighten her stockings. The latter had its rewards but in no way approached Poppa Kobe's best work.

Lunch had been arranged at a mountaintop inn that had the woodsy look of a hunting lodge. The air was surprisingly chilly and each of the tour members, including Bill and Mike, took seats at a *kotatsu*, warming their feet over the blanketed coals.

Life is certainly strange, Mike thought to himself. Short weeks ago, I was at home in the States, living a quiet life in the woods. Now I'm on a Japanese Peeping Tour, warming my feet over a *kotatsu*. And loving every minute of it, I might add.

Lunch was tangerines and sukiyaki, served by twittering junior geishas. Boisterous wartime anecdotes were told, capped off with an exhibition of nose-fighting by "Happy"

Mirimoto and a fellow twice his size. The two hopped up on the long banquet table; after a series of feints and slashes, "Happy" quickly got through to his opponent's nose, tweaking it a few times to certify his victory, but not over-doing it to the point of shaming an old comrade.

" 'Happy' was the finest nose-fighter in the Pacific," said Bill, as the squat kamikaze man accepted congratulations from his companions. "No matter how a fellow would try to protect his nose, he'd find a way to get through to it."

Though Mike enjoyed the proceedings, especially the rich feeling of camaraderie, his thoughts remained fastened on the young housewife kneeling, the girl straining at the pick-up truck, the women in the other scenes. Suddenly it occurred to him that all were one and the same. And that the single woman who had appeared in each role was Yukiko, the beautiful brain-squeezer who had been assigned to extract every last drop of Poppa Kobe's wisdom.

He asked Bill about this and his friend confirmed that it was so.

"But why would she do such a thing?" asked Mike, surprised at how disturbed he was.

"To preserve a spirit of *hommae*," said Bill. "Her position is a delicate one and it doesn't suit her purpose to upset Poppa Kobe. Besides, it probably doesn't mean that much to her."

"So she's been aware of us all along," said Mike. He wanted to add that her complicity in some way tarnished the experience, but he wasn't sure it had. Maybe it helped.

"She planned the bubble gum scene," said Bill.

"I was hoping the shopping mall was hers," said Mike, a little disappointed.

"No, that was dad's," said Bill, puffing up with pride.

"Are there any others scheduled?" asked Mike, who was torn between a desire to call it quits and another to press on.

"One more," said Bill, "and, of course, there's the wind-up at the Club."

The group finished off the lunch by singing a few military anthems which struck Mike as being on the lugubrious side. He couldn't see how they could possibly have infused the troops with a fighting spirit. But then again, there was probably no refrain that could turn clinging to atolls into an upbeat experience.

After they had left the inn, Mike spotted a man in a raincoat, behind a hedge, peering at the van through a telescope. He brought this to the attention of Bill who said the fellow was probably a private eye, hired by one of the wives to peep on the peepers.

"My guess is that it's Muriel Mirimoto," said Bill. "She has independent money and she's always been fiercely jealous of 'Happy.'

"I'd just ignore him," said Bill, hopping into the van.

Next stop on the agenda was a glade beside a waterfall. A bit lethargic after the substantial lunch, the peepers nonetheless shuffled out of the van and took up positions behind pine trees to peep at a young woman who sat beneath a tree, reading from a slim volume and stopping from time to time to recite a passage out loud. This time there was no question it was Yukiko, which made Mike feel both more and less secure at the same time. At first the tableau seemed unpromising, but then the wind pulled back a section of her black pleated skirt. Reflexively, Yukiko fidgeted a bit, shifting her panties slightly and exposing in the process a fragile, thinly tufted wisp of a vagina—

childlike and Oriental in character. Mike struggled to freeze the moment in his mind so that he could have it on file in time of need. Was this the crucial moment of his trip to Japan? If so, did it make him a less serious individual? He wondered if it were all Poppa Kobe's invention. If so, how could the retiree have been sure of the wind? Had he studied tables? Were there contingency plans, and, if so, what were they? Had Yukiko pitched in on this one? Had they run through it a few times? Whatever the case, there was no question that it was a masterstroke, a triumphant follow-up to the shopping-mall kneeling scene.

With an idle gesture—which Mike was convinced was not that idle—Yukiko rearranged her skirt, effectively bringing down the curtain on an extraordinary moment which he chose to call theatrical. Mike waited in vain for another shift in the wind and was the last one back in the van, having to be tapped on the shoulder by "Happy" Mirimoto. Possibly violating whatever convention had been established, Yukiko stood on her toes and waved good-bye to the peepers. Nonetheless, Mike waved back.

Inside the van, the lights had been switched on and the tired but happy peepers took turns congratulating Poppa Kobe on a job well done. Many of them expressed a willingness to sign on for his next tour, several insisting he accept their deposits.

Only Mike failed to take part in the merry-making.

"What's the matter, Mike?" asked Bill, slipping in beside him. "Japan getting to you?"

"It's not Japan," said Mike, who stared out of his slit and watched the rice fields go by.

The peepers were welcomed at the Club as if they had seized a heavily fortified enemy position. A swarm of plea-sure girls helped the tired tour members out of their peep-

ing clothes and into club kimonos. After first prostrating
herself before him, Suzue threw her arms around Bill and
said, somewhat preposterously, Mike thought: "Oh, Bill,
honey, I'm so glad you're safe."

Since the main body of the Club was taken up by a
Marine Plankton Symposium, the peepers were led to a
ten-mat room on the second floor of the club and served
a replenishing yakitori dinner. The manager then appeared
and delivered a brief talk on the history of the club and
the quality of its cedar furnishings. This was followed by
a solemn toast, offered by "Happy" Mirimoto, in honor of
a peeper who had died, binoculars in hand, during the
previous year's tour.

The lights were then dimmed and the fruit bowl cleared.
Taking its place was Yukiko in the brief and spangled cos-
tume of an exotic dancer. A two-piece combo slipped in
unobtrusively and started up some background music. Yukiko did a few steps, surprisingly lacking in spirit and
precision, and followed with a lazy, disinterested strip-
tease. Once she was naked, however, she brightened con-
siderably. Resting comfortably on her elbows, she flung
her astonishing legs asprawn and smiled engagingly as if
welcoming faculty members to a reception. The peepers
drew close for a better look.

Mike went downstairs to the bar and ordered a drink
from Bill's personal bottle. The bartender called upstairs
to make sure it was all right with Bill. After a short period,
Bill appeared and said, of course, to go right ahead and
serve Mike—but that Poppa Kobe was upset about his
leaving during the finale.

"He thinks you feel he didn't do a good enough job,"
said Bill, "and he's shamed."

"Tell him he did too good a job," said Mike, a remark
that Bill seemed to find confusing.

They drained Bill's personal bottle and when it was time to leave, they did not have to feign being drunk.

At the door, Bill's friend from the pleasure quarter handed Mike a note from the beautiful Todai brain-squeezer. In a magnificently calligraphed script, it said that she understood his feelings and suggested they meet at her home in the mountains.

"There I will attempt to demonstrate my position," said the note, "and to show you the real me."

The note was signed: "Fondly, Yukiko," the signature too, beautifully calligraphed.

"When did she have time to write this?" Mike asked Bill who had read the note over his shoulder.

"If she operates in the manner of *this* one," said Bill, in a cruel reference to Suzue, "she probably had a whole bunch of them printed up."

"You keep mixing me up with women who've been unkind to you," said the gentle Suzue, a remark that brought a hoglike snort from Bill.

Mike decided to let his friend's rude behavior to the lovely club girl go by for the moment—although he made a note to scold Bill about it later.

"What do you think I should do?" he asked his friend.

"I'm not sure," said Bill. "But she lives way out of the city. It'll cost you a fortune to get there."

MIKE AND HELEN ATENABE HAVE A CONVERSATION IN WHICH THEY BOTH SPEAK FROM THE HEART

THE TWO friends arrived at the Atenabe house in the middle of a commotion. As it turned out, Momma Kobe had split the cost of the private eye who had peeped on the peepers with Muriel Mirimoto. Momma Kobe knew of course that her husband had organized the tour, which he had done traditionally for many years. But the report she held in her hands said that he had done some actual peeping himself, presumably a departure from past behavior. Hands on hips, she berated him, not so much out of jealousy but for wasting his time on such foolishness.

"You can peep to your heart's content right here at home," said Momma Kobe, chasing him from one quarter of the house to the next, and smacking at him with the rolled-up report.

"Who would I peep on?" asked the harassed Poppa Kobe, trying to protect his head.

"On me, you old fool," said Momma Kobe.

"It's not the same," said Poppa Kobe, trying to find a private space.

"Because you have no imagination," said Momma Kobe, hard on his heels.

Also waiting up was Helen Atenabe, though apparently not to berate Bill but to have a late-night snack. When her husband had slipped quietly past her, with hunched shoulders, she prostrated herself before Mike, threw a fistful of salt at his face to purge him of any leftover illness and asked him to join her in a cup of bamboo soup. She seemed more trim and beautiful each time he saw her—as if she were on some kind of program.

"Tell me about Pam," she said, as she cooled off his soup, which frankly he would have preferred hot. "I've formed the impression that you get along so well."

"Pam," said Mike and realized he couldn't even say her name without smiling. And that when it came to describing her he didn't know where to start.

"I don't know *what* there is that I don't love about that woman. Take her outfits," he said, and chuckled at the thought of those weird combinations.

"She's fashionable," said Helen Atenabe, tucking her knees beneath her in the style of a little girl preparing for a bedtime story.

"Not in the conventional manner," said Mike. "But she can patch together a set of curtains and an old bandana and make it seem like a million-dollar creation. I wouldn't want to see it on anyone else, but it's her attitude that brings it off.

"She's a little careless and she's come close to killing me a few times—she leaves little traps around the house—a toaster on the floor next to my bed—we call them 'Pam-traps'—but I even love her for those. And she gets the most determined look on her face when she's out to master something—like hitting a golf ball. Bites her lip and swings the club in a slow and exaggerated way. It's not that she's so good at doing things—but she's probably better at *looking* like she can do them than anyone I ever came across. It's kind of a stylized Noh-theater way of *indicating* she's doing something rather than actually doing it, like everybody else. It's probably a little Japanese, come to think of it. She'd probably fit right in around here if it weren't for the crowds.

"And then there's her sexiness," said Mike, warming to his subject. "She'll kind of wink at me and wiggle her tush and kid the whole idea of sexiness, which of course is pretty sexy in its own right, although not officially sexy. Most people would say it isn't sexy at all. Where's the sexiness, they'd say. But I think it's just fine."

"Enough sexy," said Helen, suddenly prim. "How did you two meet?"

Her attitude put Mike on the defensive, but not for long. After all, it was a chance to talk about his fave.

"She kind of sneaked up on me. I was seeing a couple of assistant producers—not juggling them, just seeing them. And then all of a sudden, there she was, on a beach chair, next to an ornithologist. Older fellow. Nice man. Sometimes I wonder what happened to him. Anyway, the next thing I knew Pam and I were living together.

"The main thing is that I cannot get enough of that girl. Even when I'm with her all day long, I miss her, which is probably why I can go to a strange country like this with an easy head.

"I used to think there were lots of women for every man—and vice versa—but now that I'm with Pam, I honestly believe there's only one person in the world for each of us. It might take ten years or a lifetime to meet that person or you might go right through and never meet her. Thanks to some weird miracle, I met Pam."

Helen Atenabe stared off wistfully at the moon.

"Once a year," she said, trying to keep her voice steady, "Bill and I would go to the Great Bonfire on Mount Nyoi-gadake," she said. "He advertised his love for me on a balloon. We'd sit for hours and listen to *Shakuhachi* music ... But now," she said, her voice breaking, "he's even forgotten I love Szechuan food."

"I'll remind him," said Mike. "I'm sure he'll bring you all you want."

"It's too late," said Helen Atenabe. "Who knows... perhaps I should never have begun translating Japanese into Hungarian and vice versa."

"You had to follow your heart," said Mike, while privately thinking it had led her into an odd corridor.

"You're most kind," she said, half prostrating herself before him, "but I can't continue... give my best to Pam ... and leave the soup bowls for Lydia..."

With that, she slipped off to her quarters.

Mike remained at the table a while longer, letting his head clear. Perhaps it had been selfish of him to go on and on about his happiness with Pam—while Helen Atenabe's situation was so shaky. But what could he have done—misrepresent? Find deficiencies in his life at home and serve them up to her? Would that have made her feel better?

Through the paper-thin screens, he thought he heard

the sounds of an argument. Did the word *blow-job* come through the babble? Or was it just the sound of the wind chimes?

He slipped into his own area, undressed and pulled the pillow to him as if he were nestling against Pam's cozy shoulders. Yet, maddeningly, his thoughts skipped to the startled Yukiko, her skirt straining, kneeling in lace to gather up her possessions.

MIKE'S ATTEMPT TO IMPROVE PRODUCTION, WHICH LEADS TO A LUNCH WITH THE TACITURN BOARD OF DIRECTORS

THE NEXT morning, on the drive to work, Bill told Mike that things were coming to a head around the Atenabe household. Though it wasn't one hundred percent sure, the company felt it had squeezed the last bit of knowledge out of Poppa Kobe and suggested he begin actively scouting noodle shops in Tagamatsu where there was still room for a few more good ones. Several of the younger directors felt he was holding on to a few treasures for his private use and should be squeezed some more. Whatever the case, his situation was not a happy one.

Insecure about getting into Todai University, Bill Jr. was seriously considering a firm offer from a Tokyo modeling agency to scout talent on the outlying island of Hokkaido. Bill himself, as Mike well knew, was floundering on the assembly line yet unable to follow his heart and join the Yokohama Carp as an infield coach. Compounding his difficulties was increased pressure from Shigeko to pay his debts. The top Yakuza threatened to use loud-speakered trucks in Bill's neighborhood to denounce him as a welcher and deadbeat. Though devotion to the family kept her temporarily in place, Lydia, the Korean housekeeper, had been offered a high-paying job with a fast-rising group of orthodontists. Juro, the actor who boarded with the family, had agreed to do a role in a touring company of *Fiddler on the Roof*. To top it all off, Bill's wife, for the first time in their long marriage, had denied him oral sex.

"It looks like the fall of the House of Atenabe," said Bill.

Mike tried to comfort the friend who'd been so kind to him, but had to concede that Bill did have his hands full— even if they were full in a decidedly Japanese manner.

It was the plight of his son that seemed to trouble Bill the most.

"Where did I go wrong, Mike?" he asked. "Should I have spent more time cleaning his ears, taken him to Shinto shrines?"

"You really think ear-cleaning would have done the trick?" asked Mike, ignoring the shrine visits which for all he knew might have helped things along.

"You have no idea how close that brings a father and son in Japan," said Bill.

"Agents make a lot of money in our country," said Mike, trying to look on the bright side.

"Really?" said Bill, his interest quickening. "How much?"

"Ten percent of their clients' fees," said Mike. "It can add up, especially if they have one or two top acts."

"But are they revered figures?"

"Increasingly so," said Mike. "A lot of them are more revered than their clients."

"I don't know," said Bill, shaking his head. "I just don't know. And a night without oral sex...That one really hurt."

Mike said he really couldn't sympathize with Bill on that last count and suggested that in his country—perhaps due to the increasing demands on women in the marketplace—oral sex was often considered an occasional treat.

"I know you're trying to make me feel better," said the disconsolate Bill, "but don't overdo it. Next you'll recommend that I give my rife oral sex..."

"Well, what about that," said Mike, refusing to be flapped.

"Mike," said Bill, shaking his head sadly. "I thought you were supposed to be my friend."

On the assembly line that morning Mike noticed that, from time to time, stray bolts of electricity danced out of the machinery, miraculously missing the workers who went about their business as if everything were perfectly normal. Just for fun, the next time Mike saw one in his vicinity he fell back as if struck by it and began to do a kind of jerky dance around the plant, finally falling to the floor, rolling his eyes and letting his tongue hang out. Irv Miyakawa immediately threw the emergency switch, which stopped the line. A crowd of workers gathered around Mike's quivering body, the seasonals showing their concern by wringing their hands and throwing incense in his face. After a few minutes of quivering and shaking in this manner, Mike leaped to his feet, said "Ta-daaa," took a bow and indicated he had only been clowning around.

Everyone enjoyed a good laugh except Irv Miyakawa who was distressed by his antics.

"That's exactly the type of thing I mean," said Irv. "You don't take us seriously. Here we are, working our hearts out for the company, and you go and have a high old time. Then you'll leave us in the lurch and where will we be?"

"Nonsense," said Mike. "I was just trying to loosen things up around here and *help* production. Besides, all those electric shock bolts are clearly a safety hazard."

Irv conceded that Mike's predecessor had indeed been felled by a bolt of electricity, but insisted that safety standards had been tightened up since the tragic accident.

"So it wasn't just that he was a short guy," said Mike.

"What's the difference?" said Irv, defensively. "This is a pretty safe factory and you've no right to come over here and make fun of us."

Resignedly, Irv started up the assembly line. Taking a cue from Mike, the seasonals, all morning long, pretended that they, too, had been struck by electric bolts, shimmying and shaking in their positions and having the time of their lives while Irv shook his head in dismay.

Just before lunch, the Quality Control man, in a spot check, confirmed Mike's judgment by saying that the cars coming off the line did indeed have a smoother construction—although it was unlikely they would ever get past Schwartz, the top buyer from L.A. and a perfectionist.

"I'm telling you, Irv," said Mike, when the Quality Control man had completed his analysis, "the looser we get around here the better shot we have."

But Irv just mumbled something about Mike being a dilettante and not a true blue-collar fellow.

During the break, Irv and the seasonals took on a semiconductor disc unit in a tug-of-war while Bill and Mike, by special invitation, had lunch with Mr. Ito and the company's top executives.

As they washed up in the locker room, Bill said he was a little reluctant to go since he had been planning to visit a famous Old Man statue in a nearby park. He had it on good authority that the statue would come to life that very afternoon.

"Sounds like a trick to me," said Mike.

"So what," said Bill, "as long as I enjoy it."

"My very argument to you on Suzue."

"Now cut that out," said Bill, sounding remarkably like the great Jack Benny.

Mike was able to convince Bill that the meeting with Ito's Board should take precedence over the park event.

"If I know this country of yours, there'll be lots of other statues coming to life."

"That's right," said Bill. "Continue to make fun of us. Oh boy, are you in for a surprise."

Dressed in work clothes, the two friends presented a sharp contrast to the neatly dressed executives who had assembled in the director's conference room. After bows were exchanged, a document was passed from one executive to the other; each made a notation on it and then certified it with his personal seal.

"What's up?" asked Mike in a whisper.

"They're each putting down their choice for lunch," said Bill. "A decision will be made by consensus so that no one will appear to be too far out front."

"But isn't Ito the top man?"

"Yes, but it's the group that runs the company, by consensus. Normally, it would take six months to get a decision out of this committee, but everyone's pretty hungry and no question, it will go faster."

"Do they mind our whispering?" asked Mike, aware that he may have been rude.

"Not at all," said Bill. "They'll be doing a lot of it themselves throughout the meal."

A lunch of mushroom soup and baked sweet potatoes appeared to be the choice of the ten executives. Once it was prepared and placed in the center of the table, Mike reached for a portion only to have his hand smacked away by Ito.

"Now wait a bloody minute," said Mike, getting to his feet and starting to go for the company's top dog.

"Easy, Mike," said Bill, grabbing him and pulling him back to a squatting position.

"What kind of way is that to treat a guest?" Mike asked his friend.

"He's being courteous," said Bill as the company director wolfed down a few bites of each dish. "As host, it's required that he taste the food first to make sure it hasn't been poisoned."

"So it's just ceremonial, is that it?"

"Not really," said Bill. "This is a very tough business and even though Ito never gets to make any decisions, a lot of people would like to have his job."

Apart from a few low growls, the meal was eaten in silence. It was followed by a second period of silence during which Mike was tempted to say a few words, but decided he'd be damned if he would be the first to open up. After all, he and Bill were the invited guests.

After the completely wordless lunch, the executives rose and bowed to Bill and Mike and then silently filed out of the conference room.

Mr. Ito remained behind and cleaned up the table, making sure to get every last crumb before he went back to his office.

"I guess we didn't make out too well," said Mike, as the two friends returned to the assembly line.

"Not at all," said Bill. "We were a big hit."

"How can you say that?"

"What we got was a tremendous vote of confidence, Mike. They want us to keep doing what we're doing. If there'd been a lot of chattering, it would be cause for concern. But total silence is the highest compliment that group can bestow."

"I'll take your word for it," said Mike. "But they sure looked grim to me."

They watched the last part of the tug-of-war, Mike feeling a surge of pride as the tough and wiry little seasonals, led by Irv Miyakawa, yanked the opposing semiconductor group over the dividing line to victory. More and more he realized how much he had missed the camaraderie that came with being in a group. And he was beginning to feel that a key reason he had come to Japan was to find a great new bunch of fellows to hang out with.

After lunch, Mike kept after Irv Miyakawa to go along with certain measures to get the team even looser. One of the seasonals, for example, had been a rural fisherman and Irv finally agreed to let him make a weekend trip home—at company expense—to visit his old net-boss. He also gave permission to a second seasonal to keep a few barnyard animals in his dorm cubicle.

A few days later, the seasonals in question seemed completely transformed, showing up for work with new vigor and enthusiasm. Convinced he was on the right track, Mike got Irv to agree to let him use a recording of "Sweet Georgia Brown" as background music for the assembly line. Mike located a cassette in an electronics center nearby. Then he put on the catchy tape and while Bill stood by, snapping his fingers and tapping his toes, Mike rearranged the line formation, with two of the seasonals bringing the ball down, so to speak, the most agile of them handing off to Mike, who took advantage of his height to slam-dunk the top section into place. Irv's bulk was used to full advantage in clearing the boards and passing the section along to several other seasonals for final assembly. Bill was gracious enough to stand on the sidelines and act as a kind of coach, a function for which he was ideally suited. Once the team got the hang of the new procedure, the car assembly went more smoothly than ever before and Irv had to agree that they were finally getting somewhere.

"I had my doubts," said a sweating Irv, at the end of the day, "but we're gonna ram these babies down Schapiro's throat."

"Schwartz," said Mike, correcting him.

"Whatever," said Irv.

At the end of the day, the man from Quality Control inspected a few of the new elevator cars and pronounced them the finest he'd ever seen the company produce.

"If Schapiro doesn't go for them," he said, "the man's an ass."

"Schwartz," said Mike, correcting him as well.

Irv offered to stand for imported beers at a small *nawanoren* bar nearby and the group went off arm in arm as if it had won the World Series. For good luck, they stopped to urinate as a team on the factory gate and were brought up short by Shigeko, the Yakuza gambling kingpin, and a dozen of his squat and heavily muscled henchmen, who blocked their path.

"I want my dough," said Shigeko, who wore a ridiculous striped suit in the forties gangster style.

"This is all I've got," said Bill, handing over the few bills he had in his pocket.

"It's peanuts," said Shigeko, and tossed the bills to the wind. One of the seasonals started to go after them, but Irv Miyakawa held him back.

"All right, that did it," said Mike, who never did place much stock in martial arts and waded into Shigeko without another word. As it turned out, he had underestimated the top Yakuza's skills and found himself flat on his back some twenty yards away. But Irv and the tough and wiry seasonals had no such problem, tearing into the well-built but city-soft hoodlums and flinging them about as if they were chickens. Mike recovered in time to get in a few good shots, but there was no question that it was the work-hardened seasonals and the burly Irv Miyakawa who mopped up the floor with Shigeko and his team. When the battle ended, Mike got to pull himself out of the bottom of a pile. He hadn't pulled himself out of a pile in a long time and it was nice to experience the sensation again.

"A fine way to treat a veteran of the Imperial Marines," said Shigeko, his face bloodied and his gangster suit torn to ribbons.

"You were never *in* the Marines," said Irv Miyakawa. "You sat on your ass in the Ginza while the country bled."

"I was doing a lot of secret work that nobody knows about to this very day," said Shigeko. "But enough of that. My loud-speakered trucks go tomorrow."

"Your mother's kimono," said Bill, whose back seemed to have stiffened during the fight. It seemed a mild-mannered enough rejoinder, but not to judge from the look of outrage on the ganglord's face as he clenched one fist and then cowered off to join his defeated comrades.

If their accomplishments on the line had bound the unit together, the brawl did even more for their pride; Mike had to count the celebration that followed at Irv's rugged little *nawanoren* as the high point of his stay in Japan.

* * *

"I wouldn't pay Shigeko a dime," said Mike, as they drove off to Bill's club in high spirits.

"I have to," said Bill. "It's a matter of honor. Besides, if he carries though his threat to denounce me with loud-speakered trucks, I'd never be able to show my face in the neighborhood."

"Why not?" said Mike. "Your neighbors probably gamble, too."

"Not on American high-school basketball games," said Bill. "Besides, I've figured out a way to make good on my debts. Remember that apartment building right next to our house, the one that blocks out the sunlight, deprives us of fresh air and is ruining our hundred-year-old bonsai trees?"

"I think I remember it."

"The government has promised to pay us a large monthly fee for our inconvenience. Out of pride, our family has always rejected these payments. But if I accept them and turn them over to Shigeko, I think he may be satisfied. Of course, the money could go toward more instruction for Bill Jr., but as it is, he studies twenty hours a day, so it doesn't make much sense."

"Shigeko's a swine," said Mike.

"And incidentally," he continued, recalling the ease with which he'd been flung twenty yards through the air, "I wouldn't mind picking up a little of that martial arts stuff as long as I'm in Japan."

"You were blindsided," said Bill, consolingly. "Otherwise, there's no way he would have dominated you so totally."

"I'd still like to learn a few moves."

"My rife's an expert," said Bill, glumly returning to the unfortunate topic.

"Maybe you can patch things up with Helen," said Mike. "Take her to a few bonfires."

"How'd you know about those?" asked Bill suspiciously.

"She told me the other night, while we were having a snack."

"I never really cared for bonfires," said Bill. "Besides, I understand she may have a lover."

"Someone at the university?"

"No, from what I hear he's a bamboo products man from Kagashima."

"That doesn't sound like her style."

"There's a lot of money in bamboo."

"Come to think of it," said Mike, "she did offer me some bamboo soup the other night."

"Good God," said the grief-stricken Bill. "I didn't realize it had gone that far."

MIKE JOINS IN A SALUTE TO "THE BIRTHDAY BOY." THEN HIS CURIOSITY GETS THE BETTER OF HIM.

THE TWO friends stayed at the Club for a brief period on this occasion, long enough to get only mildly intoxicated and for Suzue to present Bill with a magnificently embroidered wool sweater she had knitted in her spare time.

"I wanted you to have it," she said, "in case you decide to visit the snow country this winter."

"Do I have to take you?" he asked, narrowing his already narrow eyes.

"Of course not," she said, "although you know I'd love to be with you."

Bill let out a loud cackle as they left the club.

"Wouldn't it be something if it were real," he said to

Mike, running his hand across the garment as the two men headed for the Atenabe household. It was Poppa Kobe's sixtieth birthday—one in which he got to enjoy a second childhood—and Bill had told Mike he wouldn't miss it for the world.

"But it *is* real," said Mike. "It'll keep you warm, won't it? Do you know how many hours it took to knit that thing?"

But Bill could only shake his head as if it indicate that Mike would never understand the ways of the East—no matter how much time he spent there.

For all of Bill's dire warnings about the state of the Atenabes, no outsider witnessing the tribute to Poppa Kobe would have guessed the family was experiencing the slightest difficulty. The house was gaily decorated with lanterns and good-luck charms. The birthday boy, of course, was the center of attention, dressed in diapers and red booties. Looking as flushed and trim as a new bride, Helen Atenabe fed Poppa Kobe Gerber's baby food while Momma Kobe shook rattles in his face and tickled his aging belly. In imitation of an infant playmate, "Happy" Mirimoto, Poppa Kobe's wartime comrade, crawled about on all fours and stuck out his tongue.

Lydia shook a finger at the old-timer, accusing him of being a naughty boy and showed no evidence that she was considering a lucrative job offer from a top orthodontists' group. Only Bill Jr. was missing from the festivities. Bill explained that his son had been rushed to a stomach clinic for young fellows who had studied too hard for the examinations. The doctors were trained not only to ease the pain of cramps but to continue drilling the students in mathematics as they administered treatment.

All in all, the mood was blissful. Helen looked up shyly at her husband as if she were sharing secrets with a lover. It would have been impossible to guess they were having domestic difficulties. Only Juro kept himself apart, involved as he was in mastering the difficult role of Tevye in *Fiddler on the Roof.*

Mike joined in the fun of tickling Poppa Kobe under the chin, tousling his few hairs and even attempting to get him to say "Da-da." But his participation was only halfhearted. In truth, he was unable to take his mind away from the invitation he'd received from the lovely Yukiko.

Finally, he could hold out no longer and told Bill he would be going out for a while.

"Now?" said Bill, who seemed stunned. "We're about to powder Poppa Kobe's tush."

"I really need some fresh air," said Mike. He felt bad enough betraying Pam. There was no point in involving his friend as well.

"All right," said Bill, "go right ahead. If you want to miss the high point of the ceremony."

"Take some pictures for me," said Mike, adopting a cynical tone, no doubt to compensate for the uneasiness he felt over the coming rendezvous.

Mike then bowed his way out of the house and heard a clicking sound in his lower back. To his dismay, he realized he had gotten caught in a bow and could not straighten up entirely. Nonetheless, he hunched his way along the street, taking short, mincing steps which ironically mimicked the style of the ordinary Japanese pedestrian. Feeling only moderate pain, he managed to hail a cab. After handing the driver Yukiko's address, he sat back and tried to extricate himself from the bow but saw that it was not going to be an easy job. Getting himself into a bit of a curl, he fell over on the back seat and put himself at the driver's disposal.

An hour later, Mike arrived at what appeared to be a country-style inn. Though it differed slightly in its externals, it might have belonged to the same chain as the inn he'd lunched at midway through the Peeper's Tour. After paying the driver, he winced into the reception area, there to be greeted by a young woman in ceremonial dress who seemed to be expecting him.

"I'm here to see Yukiko," he said, feeling a twinge as he said the name.

She nodded and helped him off with his shoes, replacing them with a pair of soft sandals. He caught a glimpse of some other women taking peeks at him and twittering in the corridors. The one who had greeted him led him through the main section of the inn to the edge of a perfumed garden. There she handed him another pair of sandals, indicating that they were better suited to walking through gardens. Hooked over and experiencing shooting pains in his back, he followed her along a twisted path to what appeared to be an annex; there he was presented with a pair of what he took to be special annex shoes.

"Now look," said Mike, drawing the line. "I can't keep changing shoes all the time."

"This is the last pair," said the woman.

"It better be," said Mike, slipping into them with great difficulty.

The woman led him into yet another corridor and told him to wait; then, as if by magic, she disappeared silently.

Yukiko soon appeared in much the same fashion, taking his hand and leading him along several more corridors, through screened partitions, across a heavily ornamented bridge and finally into a large shadowy room, decorated only with several rattan chairs and a bowl filled with ginko leaves shaped in the form of sparrows.

"Did you arrange these?" he asked.

"I had them brought in," she said.

"But you picked them out?" he said.

"Yes," she said, to his great relief. "And I would have arranged them if I had time. I had to rush here from work."

Mike knew, of course, that the work she had chosen to set aside was the squeezing of wisdom from loyal workers about to be forcibly retired—but for the moment he chose to ignore this.

"They're lovely," he said. "I knew you picked them out and I knew you would have arranged them if only you'd had time."

"But you're in pain," she said, noticing for the first time his awkward hooked-over stance and falling to her knees before him. "Have I done something to offend you?"

She wore a kimono splashed with a pattern of folding fans. Her hair was piled up in the ancient manner.

"Not at all," said Mike. "I got caught in a bow. It's nothing . . . It'll pass."

"We'll soon fix that," said Yukiko, helping him out of his clothing and into a night kimono and then feeding him a cup of scalding hot green tea. He allowed her to minister to him as if being undressed by a flowerlike girl were an everyday occurrence for him.

"Is it helping?" asked Yukiko.

"Quite a bit," said Mike. "I'm sure it's just nerves. It wasn't easy for me to come here."

"Did you get lost?" she asked.

"No, no," he said. "I had an excellent cab driver."

Obviously, she had misunderstood him, but he saw no reason to go into a litany about Pam and his devotion to her—an odd phrase under the circumstance. Instead, he chose to plunge right ahead with his reason for accepting her invitation. After all, it was a foreign country. There was no need to beat around the bush.

"The sight of you kneeling in the shopping mall took my breath away."

"I could feel your eyes on my body," she said, fitting one hand against his. It was half the size and perfectly molded.

"I may have exaggerated the pose a bit," she said, lowering her eyes.

"Not at all," said Mike. "It was just right. But then, when you stretched out in front of those men, I couldn't take it."

"But you were in a perfect position," said Yukiko, who seemed confused. "Lined up directly. Should I have moved closer? *Now* I know why you were upset," she said, turning away from him in tears.

"That's not it," said Mike. "I didn't want all those men staring at you."

"It was a Peeping Tour," she said, still puzzled. "What else could I have done as a finale? And those men are battle heroes. Many of them continued fighting when the war was over."

In an outburst of patriotic fervor, she clenched her fists and said: "They'd *still* be holding out if they had received the least bit of public support."

"The way you displayed yourself on that table has a whole different connotation in my country," said Mike.

"I don't care," she said with a proud toss of her head. "I plan to visit the States anyway."

"Maybe I shouldn't have come," said Mike who, despite the quirkiness of the encounter, was glad he had.

"I'm happy you did," she said, briskly changing moods. "You're so tall. I was the tallest person in my flower-arranging class, but I'm nowhere near as tall as you are."

"I'd be the shortest person in the NBA," he said, as much to himself as to Yukiko.

"Aren't you forgetting Nate "Tiny" Archibald?" she said.

Once again Mike was stunned by the average Japanese person's encyclopedic knowledge of the American sports scene.

"He's retired," said Mike.

"I'd look for a comeback," she said, further mystifying Mike with her sophistication, at least in relation to the NBA.

Yukiko excused herself and left the room. Mike noticed a sunken tub and wondered if it would help his back if he lolled around in it for a while. He also speculated on where it fit in, generally, with the evening's agenda. Soon Yukiko returned, rolling in a stringed instrument that was at least seven feet long.

"The Heain period," she said, by way of introducing her first selection. "Sad young courtiers being summoned by their ladyloves."

She then began to run from one end of the instrument to the other, plucking forth chords that sounded raucous and discordant to Mike's ears. Juro's Edo period selections had been tuneful compared to Yukiko's clatter—and with the best of intentions, it was impossible for Mike to enter into the spirit of the music. If indeed music was what had been produced. Soon Yukiko was out of breath and elected to roll the instrument into a corner.

"One of my favorite passages," she said, just as Mike had feared. "But I haven't played for a while. At my age, I should get a shorter *koto*."

"But you're just a child," said Mike, who couldn't tell if she were sixteen or twenty-six.

"Brain-squeezers age very quickly," she said, with a harsh laugh.

"I'd been wondering how you got involved in that," said Mike.

"Calligraphy was my field for many years," said Yukiko, "but when you reach a certain level of expertise, the brush tends to take on a life of its own. It was either me or the brush and since I seem to require a degree of control, I decided to give it up. My father was a tanner and there are only so many occupations open to the children of those who've touched leather. I did some catalogue modeling for the New York, New York Agency, but the opportunities are limited here in Tokyo.

"It was while I was manipulating feet at the Puppet Theater in Shibuya-ku that I learned of opportunities in the new discipline of knowledge-engineering. There weren't any barriers to people of my station. It aroused my curiosity—and it has proven to be gratifying. I've never confessed this to anyone before—perhaps only to my last boyfriend—but there is something sexual about squeezing the last drop of information out of a retiree."

"Your last boyfriend?" said Mike, fastening on perhaps the least intriguing part of her story.

"I'd rather not discuss Yosinari. He rigged pachinko machines. He had no future."

As she spoke he noticed the nape of her neck, the curve of her throat, the delicacy of her shoulders, features to which he had never paid much attention—with the possible exception of shoulders—in women he had known. Most, including Pam, God help him, had been healthy and rawboned.

"There's something I'd like to do for you, Mike," said Yukiko, leaning forward and looking at him with intensity. "Who is your favorite deceased relative?"

"That would have to be Uncle Dan," said Mike. "He died several years ago—I was much closer to him than to my own father who was a decent sort but somewhat on the cool side. Dan had a mushroom farm in California and helped subdue Pancho Villa. I was crazy about him."

"What was his *deiji?*"

"I beg your pardon," said Mike.

"His death date," said Yukiko. "Forgive me."

Mike remembered a call his uncle had put through from a medical station in Australia's remote Fifth District—a call to cheer *him* up. And then, hours later, Dan had given up the ghost.

"I think it was March...two years ago. That's as close as I can get."

"I can work with that," said Yukiko, lowering the lights and stripping to her under-kimono. It did not reveal much more of her, but it was the idea of it—Yukiko, in an under-kimono. Clasping Mike's hands, she threw back her head and made a series of guttural sounds. Then her body began to shake as if she were in the last throes of sex, although, in truth, the women Mike had known were always more modest in that situation. A crackled voice seemed to come from the walls. Where else would it have come from?

"Hiya doin', slugger. Look at the size of you, Mikey. Look at them shoulders. You're all right, kid. And don't let 'em flim-flam you, either."

And then, with a self-deprecatory laugh: "Of course *I* never did and look what it got me.

"It's not too bad up here," the voice continued, "a day is a day, just like everywhere else. Just don't expect any *foie gras.* I miss you, Mike. And don't waste your tears on Danny. Although I have to admit, they *did* lay a glove on me."

The voice, though tinny in the style of an old recording, bore a remarkable similarity to that of Mike's favorite uncle, in both pitch and intonation. Had Yukiko really been able to summon him up from the dead? Taking the darkest possible view, even if she had a girlfriend working with her in the next room—and this was an awful thing to suspect her of—what a remarkable job of research it must have required to capture Dan's style with such accuracy. The gentle gruffness, the flip sentimentaility. What could they have worked with—old snapshots? A sense they got of him from secretly observing Mike?

On the other hand, the elegiac words lacked specificity and could have been spoken by a wide variety of uncles. Everyone had a hell-for-leather type in the family who had left home in search of adventure. A gifted impersonator had only to work up an overall uncle routine and then dub in a few proper names to fit the individual case. "Mike" and "Danny Boy" in this instance. Was it possible that a long line of visiting Yanks had been moved by the identical speech? Mike thought he heard a feathery drumbeat of footsteps behind the wall and became convinced that Yukiko had worked with a cohort. Possibly the woman who had supplied him with garden and annex shoes. None of this fazed him. The mimicry had been dazzling. And once again, Mike was impressed by the inventiveness of the Japanese, which obviously ranged far beyond the purely technological. Would his own country have bothered to serve up Uncle Dan? Would it have realized how important it was for him to make contact with the old scoundrel? Even if the technique was a little fraudulent? Japan did.

Yukiko trembled more violently than ever. Finally, she

stopped, turned the lights back on and fell to the ground.

"That was a tough one," she said.

"I can imagine," said Mike, cradling her in his arms, secretly inhaling her fragrance and giving no indication he was on to what might have been an attractive scam.

When she had recovered her strength, Yukiko asked Mike if he would like her to try on some Noh masks.

"They show the full range of human emotion."

"I don't believe so," said Mike. "Quite frankly, I've had an awful lot of culture thrown at me in a short space of time."

"May I bathe you?" she asked.

"Absolutely."

When they had removed their kimonos and held each other in the sunken bath, Yukiko asked Mike if he was sure he wouldn't prefer a geisha.

"I'm positive," said Mike, hardly daring to look at her.

"I'm glad," said Yukiko who suddenly sunk her teeth so deeply into Mike's shoulder he was sure she had touched bone. The effect was electrifying; it was all he could do to keep from crushing her. Instead, trying to ignore his back, he carried her to a mat and set her down gently beside him.

"What I'd like to know," he said, feeling around for the pain, "is who asked me to do all that bowing?"

"It's so obviously symbolic," she said,

"Maybe, but it hurts like hell."

"Try some Ladies' Liqueur," she said, pouring a thimbleful from a cut-glass decanter and dimming the lights. He swallowed it in one gulp. He thought he heard her say something about sipping it, but her voice now came from a far-off chamber, along with a jovial echoing toast from his Uncle Dan:

"Here's lookin at ya', kid."

The fragrance of the perfumed garden filled the room. He remembered Yukiko in dizzying pretzellike positions. Or was it possibly a lookalike, the woman who had greeted him and supplied him with annex shoes? What purpose would that have served? He imagined that whoever it was had knelt again for him, legs straining, hopelessly gathering up possessions. Had he gotten his reward? Lips pressed against that thin and scented dividing wisp? And then he remembered white-powdered cheeks and black teeth and a scream.

When he awakened, Yukiko had raised the shades and was fully dressed, in Western clothing, standing beside a bay window. He looked at his watch and saw that he was late for work.

"What happened, Mike?" she asked. "You seemed to draw away toward daylight."

"I'm not sure," he said. "I think the black teeth may have thrown me a bit."

"But that was to please you," she said. "Men secretly long for it. Few women are bold enough to comply."

"It probably takes a little getting used to," he said.

"The dye will wear off in a day or two."

"Then I'll drop back. Meanwhile, I wonder if you'd call a cab for me."

"As you like," she said, prostrating herself before him, Western clothes and all, and then slipping off to make the arrangements.

Mike's back was so bad he could hardly get dressed. He seemed to be in a full bow now, the kind used to signify events of enormous gravity, like the signing of treaties.

"He'll be here in fifteen minutes," said Yukiko, upon her return. "I've ordered scrambled eggs and bacon for you, but I think it's best that we take separate cabs."

"I appreciate everything you've done, Yukiko."

"It was nothing," she said as she prepared to leave. "But I do hope you come back, Mike. I'd hate to think of you as just another Japanophile."

A TEMPORARY VICTORY FOLLOWED BY A SHOCKING DECISION ON THE PART OF BILL

WAS THAT what he was, a serious dilettante? Mike wondered about this as the cab took him directly to the factory. Yukiko had implied as much and so, for that matter, had Irv Miyakawa. Make a quick hit, sponge up the culture, tease around a little bit and then be on your way.

But if this was so, why was he rushing back to the factory? It certainly wasn't the peanuts he was earning on the line. For all he knew, his own house-restoring business had gone down the drain and he would have to start over. And why was he was unwilling to desert Irv and Bill and the seasonals? Was that the style of a tease? And how about the powerful ties he felt to the Antenabes? It was as if they

161

were his own family. Would a casual man feel this way?

As to his being thrown off stride by Yukiko's white-powdered cheeks and black teeth—was that his fault? What was he supposed to do, forget about Pam and live out his life with a black-toothed woman—just to prove he wasn't a dilettante?

And as for Pam, he felt bad enough about his treachery toward her, even though he wasn't quite sure exactly what he had done in the darkness of the inn. For all he knew, he had rolled around with an impostor, not that it would mitigate his behavior. His crime, if any, was that he had unquestionably been drawn to Yukiko. (Whether he'd be able to rekindle this attraction after the teeth was another story.) He still loved Pam but knew that he would have a tough time telling her about Yukiko. And normally, he shared all his adventures with her. Eventually, he would probably share this one with her, too, although it was important to get it exactly right, putting Yukiko in the proper context.

Meanwhile, his tongue was thick, he was still hooked over in a formal bow, and he felt absolutely awful about showing up late at the factory in the same clothes he'd worn the day before. He thought of nights he'd behaved disgracefully, fully expecting to be crushed at daylight by a powerful blow. More often than not, ironically, he had been greeted by a cloudburst of good news. He hoped that this would be the case once again as he slipped back onto the line and tried to behave inconspicuously.

It wasn't necessary for him to hunch over his shoulders since he was all hooked over in a bow anyway. Irv shook his head as if to confirm that Mike had let down the team—and that his deceit came as no surprise. Even the seasonals averted their eyes. In place of the rhythm-and-blues tapes

that had worked so effectively to loosen up the team, Irv
Miyakawa had substituted a musical salute to the Ito Company. Obviously, this was designed as an affront to Mike
who couldn't possibly be expected to know the lyrics. The
new background music, coupled with the fact that he was
still trapped in a bow, threw off Mike's rhythm badly. So
much so that he put two elevator tops on backwards, further heightening the scorn of Irv and the once-beloved
seasonals. Suddenly, Mike didn't like the pasty-faced supervisor that much anymore. Who was he to go around
passing judgment on an American? Mike couldn't bring
himself to dislike the seasonals, but he was disappointed
in the way they fell in step against him. And where, incidentally, was Bill Atenabe when he needed him? Exactly
where you'd expect a Jap to be when you were backed
against a wall. Nowhere.

Eating his noodles in the rain, Mike knew what it was
to be alone in a strange land—although he'd felt a little
bit the same way in Finland, come to think of it.

But then, just as he was about to pack it in and go back
to the beloved country of his origin, Irv came running out
to greet him with the news that Schwartz had okayed the
most recent run of elevator cars. A shipment of them had
already been diverted from Singapore and sent to the West
Coast. This meant that Mr. Ito would finally realize his
dream of having his cars running in downtown L.A. In
addition, Schwartz planned to use one of the smooth-
functioning cars for his own condo in the heart of Beverly
Hills. And he sent his personal congratulations to the
American Jew who had made it all possible.

"Who's that?" asked the puzzled Mike who had come
out of his bow without realizing it.

"Aren't you Jewish?" asked Irv.

"No," said Mike. "Am I supposed to be?"

"Ito and Schwartz assumed you were. Do you have any relatives in Laguna Beach?"

"No," said Mike.

"I see," said Irv, looking a little confused. "Well, what do we do with all the chicken soup we ordered for the celebration?"

"We'll eat it," said Mike. "One thing has nothing to do with another. Meanwhile, I'm concerned about Bill. It isn't like him to just not show up this way."

"Tell him that if he has any personal problems and feels like spilling his guts..."

"I'm afraid he's past that," said Mike. "I better call him."

"Take the afternoon off if you have to," said Irv. "And listen, thanks for hanging in there with us. Ito is switching our unit over to his troubled suitcase division. It's a great compliment, actually. Can we count on you, Mike, to help turn it around?"

Careful not to do any serious bowing, Mike lowered his head cautiously and said he'd certainly consider it. But for the moment, he was more concerned about his pal Bill.

Using a company phone, he rang up his friend and got no answer, not even a recorded message from the Atenabe answering machine. So he decided to take a cab out there, not even blinking when the driver said he'd have to charge him twice the meter—since the Atenabes were beyond the primary driving circle.

With disaster in the air, Mike tried to distract himself by thinking of ways to bolster the ailing suitcase division. The arrival of a fresh team would be helpful, in and of itself. But what about suitcases with built-in computers and video cassette equipment? And plenty of room left over for suits and ties. They would have to be awfully sturdy but maybe it was worth a try. If the company engineers hadn't thought of it yet. Or how about a gadget that pressed your pants while you flew? Congratulating himself perhaps a shade too vigorously, Mike began to feel that maybe he did have a little Japanese in him. And that it was no accident he had just picked up one day and flown over there. None of which meant he was about to turn his back on Pam and his old country. Far from it.

And then, next thing he knew, he was racing across the tiny, immaculately designed garden of the Atenabes, with suitcases the furthest thing from his mind.

What he saw when he entered the house was far from encouraging—Poppa Kobe, bent over, head in his hands, in the style of a Soviet dissident who'd just been refused a passport. And standing over him, Yukiko, in a tight black skirt, short mink stole and stiletto heels, berating the old-timer for not divulging some last bit of wisdom she believed he was clinging to for personal reasons. Her hair was frizzed—he never dreamed she could be so cold-looking. Had it been the short-lived romance with Mike that had turned her hard and calculating? Or was it presumptuous of him to think so? How could she have been so delicate and yielding the night before? Even her long legs didn't look that great, although, in truth, they weren't that bad either. Perhaps this was a wicked sister and not Yukiko. If so, he didn't care for either one of them. Pulling her away from Poppa Kobe, Mike told Yukiko to lay off the old man.

"It's none of your business," she said, defiantly, "This is not your country and it never will be."

"That may be," said Mike, "but I know suffering and I'm not putting up with it."

"What about Negroes in the South?" she shouted at him.

"You're behind the times," said Mike. "They're making great strides."

He tried to lead Poppa Kobe away. At first the old man resisted, throwing up a fist, but then, wearily, he allowed himself to be led off to the kitchen. There, Momma Kobe sat impassively. She, too, seemed to have lost her vitality.

Mike advised Poppa Kobe not to cooperate further with Yukiko. Somehow, though no one had asked him, he felt a need to take charge.

"You've given that company enough," he said, "and you're entitled to save a little something for yourself."

"Didn't I tell you that?" said Momma Kobe, nudging her husband. She seemed to have aged dramatically overnight.

Some instinct then led Mike to the teahouse. Tearing through the garden, he forgot all about his back and entered the structure on all fours. There he found Bill, who'd laid out a ceremonial mat and was sharpening two swords, one long, the other short.

"It's all over, Mike," said Bill. "Bill Jr. flunked his examination for Todai and Helen left me last night. She took all of our possessions, including the electric futon."

"The bamboo products man?" said Mike.

"No, this fellow's in teak. I had the bamboo person all wrong and wrote him a note of apology. In any case, my whole world's come apart. You saw what they did to Poppa Kobe. There's just too much for me to handle. So I've decided to commit *seppuku*. I thought about the Aokigahara Forest as a possible site, but it's become more crowded than the Ginza. So I plan to do it right here.

"And Mike," he said shyly, touching his friend's arm. "I want you to be my *kaishaku*."

"What's that?"

"My witness and assistant."

"But I couldn't possibly do that."

"I'm not asking you to kill me, Mike. I'll be dead already. After I run the dagger through my belly, you chop my head off. It would mean a great deal to me, Mike. You're my closest friend."

"Out of the question, Bill. It's totally alien to everything I am and everything I've ever done."

"I'm surprised at you, Mike. And not a little disappointed. I should have known—once a *gaijin*, always a *gaijin*."

"I've had quite enough of that," said Mike. "*Gaijin*, dilettante, tease, fair-weather friend. I don't think I've been the worst guy in the world around here. I'd like to see you live to a ripe old age, Bill. Doesn't that count for something?"

"It's a bit of betrayal, Mike."

"But you've got so much to live for."

"For instance," said Bill.

"I don't even know where to start."

"Neither do I."

"There's Bill Jr.," said Mike. "Admittedly, he wants to be a modeling agent, but as I've pointed out, there are some fine people in that profession. And what about Suzue? You may see her as an insincere pleasure girl, but she's crazy about you."

"You're grasping at straws," said Bill. "Just look what they've done to my poor father."

"There's obviously one piece of information he won't divulge, although I have to admit they're being obnoxious in the way they're trying to get it."

"Yukiko's a flirt."

"She's more than a flirt. In any case, I'll call Ito and find out what the company wants from Poppa Kobe. Maybe we can strike a deal. Our unit, incidentally, got the elevator contract for downtown L.A. which is another thing you might be proud of."

"I didn't participate," said Bill.

"You did in spirit. Anyway, Ito owes us something. Now for God's sake, Bill, take heart. How many guys are sitting around with a firm offer to be a player-coach for the Hiroshima Carp?"

"Oh sure," said Bill, dismissively. "But have I heard one word from the Nippon Ham Fighters? It's no use. I'm committed to *seppuku*. You may think it's awful, but it's part of a long and honorable tradition. At least ten of our finest writers, including two Nobel Prize winners, have died by their own hand—so there must be something to it."

Suddenly, the reality of Bill's plan hit Mike. Someone who had befriended him and treated him like a brother was about to take his own life. Perhaps in Japan this was nobody's business, but Mike was there on a temporary basis.

"I'm not letting you do it," said Mike, advancing on his friend.

"You'll have to kill me," said Bill, suddenly revived and taking up the short knife.

Finally, Mike saw that Bill wasn't putting on a show; his friend was resigned to his fate and didn't see anything disagreeable about it. In addition, there was no point in killing him to keep him from killing himself.

"When do you plan to do this?" asked Mike.

"Does this mean you'll be my *kaishaku?*" Before Mike could answer, Bill smacked a fist into his palm as if he'd found a backer for a new show.

"I'll think it over," said Mike, not adding that if he did so for a thousand years there was no way he was going to chop off his friend's head—even if he was dead already. He had always prided himself on keeping an open mind— but this was pushing him to the wall.

"There's no rush," said Bill, "although I would like to jump on it as soon as possible. And it's important to get it right. I have to buy a new loincloth and get my white kimono over to the dry cleaners. I've already picked out my Buddhist death name—Yamaguchi—but I've got to have some commemorative photographs taken and clean up the place. There are the farewell notes, my address to the empire, the keepsakes—I hadn't realized there was so much to do. If I really move fast, I should be ready to go by midnight."

"I'd offer to help," said Mike, idiotically.

"That's all right," said Bill, going back to his swords. "But please let me get started."

Just then, Momma Kobe poked her head into the tea- house and said there was a call for Mike from Pam. Much as he loved her and was happy to hear she was on the line, frankly that was the last thing he needed, a phone call. Nonetheless, he excused himself and raced into the main area of the house. Chances were, Bill would be safe for the moment in his mother's hands, although Momma Kobe seemed to be taking a remarkably tranquil attitude toward her son's planned suicide. Perhaps that was the way in Japan—never meddle in a son's affairs.

"Pam," said Mike. "I'm under a little heat at the mo- ment. Can I call you back later?"

"I might not be in," said Pam.

"What do you mean?" he said, panicked. Even though it was Pam, it was still a chilling line.

"Honey, I just can't take being away from you anymore. I love you, but I'm just not that kind of person. I miss you too much, so I've decided to spend a few days with Sheila."

"The crazy one?" said Mike. "Doesn't she give wild parties? Didn't they drag you across the carpeting one night?"

"That was years ago, honey."

"Pam, how can you do a thing like that? You know I can't take change. There's a friend of mine who's about to commit *seppuku*. And now I have to worry about you being dragged across the carpeting."

"Nobody's going to drag me across the carpeting, Mike. And I'm sorry about your friend. But I just can't stand being alone anymore. I'll give you Sheila's number."

"All right, Pam," he said, reaching for a pencil. "But you're not really helping."

MIKE TO THE
RESCUE

AFTER HE'D hung up, Mike couldn't decide whether to stay with Bill or race off and find Suzue, whom he considered his best bet. Even though Bill was contemptuous of the magnificent pleasure girl, perhaps the sight of her in fresh environment would shock him back to his senses. A psychiatrist was another possibility, but for all he knew, the shrinks in this strange country would probably tell you to go ahead and kill yourself if it made you feel better.

So once again, he raced into the street and flagged down a cab. The fares by this time were destroying him, reason alone to head back to the States. On the other hand, maybe he could justify the travel as a business expense. If Bill killed himself in his absence, Mike would always have it on his conscience, even though he was morally covered in that he was only deserting his friend to help him. And what could he do to stop him, wrestle him for the swords and wind up with one of them in his own belly? That would really be serious. Besides, although technically deranged, at least by Western standards, Bill would probably keep his word and not kill himself until midnight. The teahouse was a mess. It would take hours to get it cleaned up. Even if he found a same-day dry cleaner, it would take some time to get the spots out of his kimono.

Mike tried to relax as he sped off toward the Club.

Once he was there, the manager said that Suzue wouldn't be in for a few hours and that he was sorry, he had no authorization to let Mike have a drink of Bill's private whiskey.

"I don't *want* his whiskey," said Mike. "What's wrong with you people? The guy is about to commit *seppuku.*"

"I'm sorry to hear that," said the manager, with a little bow. "Why don't you have a drink of mine?"

Mike took the fellow up on his offer. To kill time, he listened in on an afternoon rice symposium. Then he put through a call to Ito, who confirmed that there was, indeed, one last bit of wisdom the company wanted from Poppa Kobe before it forcibly retired him.

"While he was working for us, he came up with a formula for a mile-long noodle. We're anxious to have that before we say good-bye to him."

"Oh for Christ's sake," said Mike, who by this time had had his bellyful of the Japanese style. "Clearly, he's devised this to help him in his own retirement. Something to set his place off from the other noodle shops. Why don't you give the poor guy a break?"

"Technically speaking, you're incorrect," said Ito. "But I read you and you may have a point. I'll take it up with my colleagues, although it could take a couple of months to get a decision."

"He may be dead then."

"Touché, Mike. I'll see what I can do to speed things up. Thanks again for your help and, once again, Schwartz says hello."

"Tell him hi from me," said Mike and hung up.

With Ito in his pocket, Mike felt a little better. At least he'd have a bone to throw to his friend. But would Bill change his plan just because his father was assured of a chance to live out his life selling mile-long noodles? It hardly seemed likely. For all he knew, Bill might be dead already. A siren went off in his head as he put through a call to his friend. Instead of Bill, he got through to Momma Kobe, who said that her son was fine, a little pale perhaps, but otherwise nothing unusual. What really disturbed her was that Lydia had left, taking an apartment in the typhoon country so she could be closer to her son.

"And she took my pots, too, that lousy Korean."

Mike scolded her for adopting the same racial attitudes as the police whom she had always scorned.

"You may be right," said Momma Kobe. "But still . . . my pots."

"Worry about your son," said Mike. "He's the one who needs help."

"He's a grown man," said Momma Kobe. "If he doesn't know what's good for him, he never will."

In one sense it was hard to argue with that kind of logic, especially with a Japanese person, so Mike, once again idiotically, told her to hang in, he'd be back as soon as possible.

The manager at the Club bar seemed to sense Mike's distress. His style became gentle.

"How about a game of mah-jongg to pass the time," he said. "Often it's harder on those who stand by. And we don't have to play for money."

Mike thanked him for his consideration and took him up on his offer. But by the time the tiles were in place, Suzue appeared. Wearing a western street dress, she seemed a simple person with a slender and honest body, a far cry from the glamorous night creature he'd met before. Although her legs were terrific, even in daylight.

"Suzue," said Mike. "Bill's wife left him and he's about to commit *seppuku*. I have a feeling you're the only one who can stop him. I know you love Bill and I was there when you offered to share your life with him in Kyoto.

"Don't be absurd," said Suzue. "That was just rhetoric."

"So Bill was right," said Mike, astonished by her response. "You *are* just a pleasure woman."

"I never pretended otherwise," said Suzue, climbing the stairs to her dressing room.

Mike couldn't get over how badly he'd been fooled. The whole country kept fooling him. Never for a second had he doubted the strength of Suzue's feeling for Bill.

"I'm a professional," she said, when she reached the landing. "Every waking moment of my life has been thrown over to creating illusion. Few have done it better. Does he think I've been waiting for him to come along and snap his fingers so that I can trivialize everything I've worked to achieve?"

Mike tried to relate her situation to his work in house-restoring and began to get a glimmer of understanding.

"The audacity," she hissed and then threw back her head, producing a strange trumpeting sound of either ag-

ony or triumph—he couldn't tell which. But it further
confirmed his feeling that the emotional gulf between East
and West was unbridgeable. He wouldn't know, for example, whether to comfort such a person or join her in
exultation.

But then, on more familiar ground, she said: "Perhaps
I can balance two careers. Do you think he'd put up with
my cats?"

Mike ran up the stairs and hugged Suzue when she said
this. For a second he forgot she was Bill's girl. But then
he quickly came to his senses and off he raced again, to
the Atenabe household, with Suzue at the wheel of her
Datsun, driving in perfect British racing-car style. Mike
was delighted to be able to give her impeccable directions.
She drove as if they were going to a fire—and, of course,
in many ways it was worse than a fire.

Holding Suzue's hand, not that she needed help, Mike
tore through the empty main section of the home and
reached the teahouse. A foreign smell brought him up
short, one that he could only identify as being *real*. What
he saw next was worse than anything he had ever come
across, and that included a mercifully brief tour in 'Nam—
a head rolling toward him.

Automatically, he stepped aside as if he were playing
dodgeball. Fortunately, it wasn't Bill's head, although it
did look familiar. Only when it came to rest at the foot of
a maple tree did he recognize it as belonging to "Happy"
Mirimoto, marked as it was by a big smile.

A shaken and trembling Bill came out and quickly explained.

"I had a premonition that you wouldn't come, Mike, so
I called "Happy" Mirimoto. He lives nearby and he's the

only one I could get to fill in as my *kaishaku* on such short notice. I was about to fall on my short sword when "Happy" got a funny look on his face and shoved me aside. Then he fell on it himself. I had no recourse but to chop off his head. But I wouldn't worry about "Happy." All through the war, as you know, he tried and tried to pull off a successful kamikaze raid and failed."

"Obviously, he finally got his wish."

"You're not going to follow him, are you?" said Mike, moving discreetly away from the head.

"Are you crazy?" said Bill. "This is the most violent thing I've ever seen. I had no idea. It's worse than a dozen car crashes. I wouldn't dream of it.

"Let's get out of here," he continued. "Happy's friends are coming to take him to the Imperial Cemetery. The feeling I get is that they're prouder of him than ever."

A FOND FAREWELL

ONLY WHEN they had gone back to the main house did Bill seem to become aware of Suzue.

"What are you doing here?" he asked, not altogether displeased. "You look so different in the daylight."

"I heard that you'd been abandoned and were about to commit *seppuko*. I know you think I'm a fraud, but I want you to come and stay with me in Kyoto. I'll be very quiet and you'll never even notice me."

"But what about your work?" asked Bill.

"I'll give it up if you like—or I'll put in three nights a week and see how it works out."

"I'd take her up on it," said Mike. "Even if it turns out

to be an illusion, it'll be a terrific illusion."

"Those are strong words," said Bill, not specifying which ones he meant. "I don't know if I'm ready for a permanent relationship."

"I'll tell you what'll help," said Mike, surprised at the ease with which he was tossing off advice. "Tell Helen you want your electric futon back."

"Dammit," said Bill, his back straightening. "Why didn't I think of that?"

But then his shoulders sagged and he said: "How could Helen have done that to me?"

"She did it, that's the main thing," said Mike. "It was probably building up for a long time."

"Well, I'm not out of the woods by a long shot. I can sense I'm going to have trouble getting a full night's sleep. And right this moment I have no sexual energy."

"We can forget living in Kyoto for the time being," said Suzue, "and just cuddle for a few weekends in Nikko."

"Not a bad idea," said Bill. Easily and naturally, he put his arm around Suzue's shoulders.

"I have a small trust fund," she said, "to settle your debt to Shigeko."

"That won't be necessary," said Bill. "As part of my preparation for committing *seppuku*, I made a huge bet on Saint Agnes High School of Long Island against powerful Port Jefferson. In a way, it was cowardly of me. If I lost, the Atenabe family would have to pay off my debt with its few remaining hectares. And, of course, I would be out of the picture. But somehow I smelled upset and sure enough, Saint Agnes won handily. As a result, Shigeko has already called off the loudspeakered trucks that were besmirching my name in the neighborhood."

"Will you come and stay with us?" Suzue asked Mike,

almost unnoticeably changing the subject.

"I don't think so. I've crammed an awful lot into my stay here. I think it's time I got on my horse."

What Mike didn't tell them was that he had had enough of this appealing and yet maddening country. The tea-houses, the funeral urns, the rain celebrations, black teeth, powdered cheeks. The head had just about driven him 'round the bend.

"But you and Pam will visit us someday?" said Suzue.

"Without question," said Mike, who somehow had the feeling that they wouldn't. He'd made that promise to a couple of Finns once, and they were still waiting for him. When Mike said good-bye, he meant it.

"So it's hi-yo, Silver, eh, Mike," said Bill with the amiable chuckle Mike had found so appealing on the plane.

"'Fraid so, partner," said Mike.

The two friends embraced each other without shame.

"I'm getting very 'motional," said Bill.

To Mike's recollection, it was only the second time a word had forced Bill back into pidgin. Again, it was un-questionably the strength of his feelings which had pro-duced the minor lapse.

Momma and Poppa Kobe slid back their shoji screens and Mike said good-bye to them as well, thanking the two old-timers for their hospitality and wishing Poppa Kobe good luck with his mile-long noodle shop in Yokohama. Then he hugged Momma Kobe who said that Bill Jr. had gotten off to a good start in the agency business, having signed Yukiko as his first client.

"I'm surprised she left brain-squeezing so abruptly," said Mike.

"Modeling was always her first love," said Momma Kobe. "All she needed was a first-rate agent."

Bill told Mike he would make his apologies and send his regards to Mr. Ito and Irv Miyakawa. Mike in turn had Bill promise to send his special good wishes to the seasonals. What was it about those fellows? And why had he come to love them so much when, apart from a couple of lunches in the rain, he hadn't really spent that much time with them? Was it because they worked a season and then silently slipped off to their farms without causing trouble? Whatever the case, they were the salt of the earth, Japanwise, as far as Mike was concerned, and he knew he was going to miss them.

Using his last shred of influence, Poppa Kobe was able to round up a company car to take Mike to Haneda Airport. Next thing he knew, with almost sleight-of-hand speed, Mike was staring out at the Pacific, on his way to San Francisco.

Had he left too abruptly? In many ways, it wasn't Japan he had fallen in love with so much as the Atenabe family. And in that sense, his work, so to speak, was at an end. The House of Atenabe was no more, although it would no doubt continue to exist in other incarnations. As far as he could see, the house itself would be sold along with all the remaining hectares. He had been there in the last stages. Was that his role in life, to preside over the disintegration of families, after first making sure that each member was sturdy and able to face being scattered? If so, it was some job. Maybe it was time for him and Pam to start a family of their own.

These were Mike's thoughts as he journeyed back to the States. He was melancholy; at the same time, he wanted to whip the plane to make it go faster. *Speed and melancholy.* Had he become irrevocably Japanese?

* * *

At the terminal he called Pam at Sheila's house and there was no answer. Were they all drugged out, he wondered. Then he called her at home, which was where she was.

"What happened to Sheila?" he asked.

"She's fine," said Pam. "We had a good gossip and then I couldn't stand to be away from you—even though you weren't here."

"Not to fear, babe. I'm in San Francisco."

"You are?" she said, excited. "You didn't leave because of something I said, did you?"

"No, hon, I'm finished up."

"Tell me what happened."

"Not on the phone, babe. I'd be talking for two weeks."

"Well, HURRY UP," she said. "And you know why."

He could tell she was making her mischief face. Just his luck he would die on the plane.

To while away the time between flights, Mike called a friend who lived in the area. He could have called any old time, but being close by was what gave him the idea. They had gone to college together. The friend made a fortune of money as an investment banker, but had never married. He had gone out with one woman after another but somehow he had never found one to live with. Nor did he come across gay. He told Mike that his mother, who lived nearby, was dying. And he had given up all hope of meeting the right person. So he stayed home alone in a huge dark house and watched video cassettes. When he tired of them, he did old comedy routines aloud, ones he had been known for at college. He did all the parts and he did them for his own benefit, in a dark empty living room. He had been a cheerleader at college. Sometimes, late at night, he did his cheers, too, for an invisible stadium crowd.

He told all of this to Mike on the phone and when he

was finished, Mike said: "I'm sorry, but I've just come off a big one and I can't take your case."

And then he flew back east, got a boost for his car battery and was soon driving up the driveway, all in what seemed like one smooth, continuous motion.

HOME AGAIN

FRESH CRISP apples were on the trees and all over the ground. He had missed out on the white peaches, all except for a single plump one that still clung stubbornly to a branch as if waiting for his return. Mort didn't bark. He knew better. He just sat there, framed by the living-room window, alert and quivering as if he were auditioning for a dog food commercial. Something was dramatically different about the house, although there was no question that he had come to the right place. Through the giant panes he saw lanterns strung along the rafters. A wreath made of pine boughs and bamboo hung above the mantlepiece. The smell of incense floated through the screen door.

Had he missed a turn and gone back to the Atenabes?

Inside, Mort was the first to greet him, a leaping, lapping
Lab. Pam stood by, waiting for the production to end. She
wore a kimono, her hair brushed up in a bun with an ivory
comb stuck through it. She looked fresh-faced and rested
and trim and he would have grabbed her and gone at it
right there if she hadn't pushed him off and screamed,
"Wait, wait, wait a bloody minute" as if the house were
on fire. She always frightened him when she did that; this
time, too, he drew back with a tight stomach. The out-
bursts were some kind of holdover from sixties political
rallies when she had to rush up on platforms and shout
something to the crowd.

On this occasion, she prostrated herself before him with
great solemnity and said, *"Moshi, moshi,* Mike. *Hirasha
maise."*

"Excellent," he said, and it was. He hadn't seen a better
ceremonial move in Japan itself. It was fine except for the
accent. Pam was a brilliant actress who did the world's
worst dialects, all of them sounding a little Central Euro-
pean with some vaudeville thrown in. Her Japanese, too,
was straight out of Central Europe, which was no small
accomplishment.

"Thank you, Mike," she said. "Now take those shoes
off before we get ten years of bad luck."

She started to tug at his moccasins.

"All right, Pam," he said, helping her to her feet.

"What's wrong, Mike?" she said, all eyes and innocence.
"This is your reentry. You'll probably want to get into a
fresh kimono. I got you two beauties. They were on sale
at the new Gertz."

"And look," she said, pointing to the dining-room table.
"Tuna sashimi, fresh from the dock. One tuna came in
with a swordfish catch and I got you a side of it."

"What are you going to eat?"

"Oh, I don't know, I'll find something."

"Bologna?"

"No," she said, hands on her hips, palms facing backward. "I'm not going to eat any bologna."

She smacked him around a little, which he enjoyed.

"You probably told everyone in Japan I was a bologna queen."

"Just a few people."

"You're awful," she said. "Now come on upstairs. I was just assembling one of those straw mats. You'll know how to help me."

"Pam," he said.

"What, Mike? You're Japaned out?"

She said this last as if the idea had just hit her.

"Well then, you just relax and let me pour you a great big delicious drink. Are you hungry, Mike? I got some ribs as a backup."

"Just the drink, babe."

He settled into the couch and looked around at the house he enjoyed so much. He told everyone he had bought it in five minutes after looking at fifty and it was more or less true. No matter where you sat, you could look out and see something that made you feel better. He wondered what in the world had ever possessed him to leave. And now there was a whole patch of time without Pam that could never be made up. And never mind how much the trip had enriched him, with Pam in line for the spillover benefits.

She brought him a tumbler of scotch and shook out her hair. It seemed to have gotten thicker in the time he was away.

"Well, did you at least have a great time, you goof?"

"I'm not sure," he said. "I just want to think about it

for a while and not say anything before I make up my mind."

"Do whatever makes you happy, babe."

"I appreciate that," he said, and went ahead and told her the whole story anyway, even throwing in some once-over-lightly coverage of Yukiko. But mostly he stuck to the Atenabes, the way he had moved in with them, gotten involved in their fortunes and then had to say good-bye, all in such a short space of time. He said he hadn't realized how much he missed having a family, his own having died off without any fanfare. Pam reminded him of his cousin, who was a marine biologist in Key West, and Mike had to agree that yes, Hank was an agreeable enough fellow but hardly the stuff of a tight hereditary unit. Pam held his hands and told him not to worry since they might very well have started one of their own. He asked her what she meant and why she hadn't told him about it. She said she hadn't been too sure at the time and saw no reason to spoil his good time. He reminded her that he still wasn't sure he'd had one. Then he said "For God's sake" a few times, which didn't seem to accomplish anything. So he reached for her. She drew back and said: "Just like that? No preliminaries?"

"You smell nice," he said.

"Oh, great," she said. "Dear mom, guess what? Mike just came back from Japan and said I smelled nice. Isn't he some guy? Love, Pam.

"C'mon, big fella. You've been away for a long time and I'm shy."

"I'm shy, too,' he said. "You know I'm a shy sonofa-bitch."

And the funny thing is, he was. She got him that way. They could spend a couple of hours rolling around on the carpeting and the next time up, he'd be shy again.

But it didn't stop him from grabbing her and telling her he loved her and kissing her face off. He took off her kimono and wondered how it was possible for her to be so lean and mean in her condition. But that's probably the way it would work—until she took off in the other direction. He admired the Frederick's of Hollywood panties that she had finally gotten around to wearing—although he wasn't sure they went with the kimono. Then he kissed her and swore that if he ever got one of his urges again he would never repeat never yield to it until he had done everything humanly possible to try to work her in on it. An offer, incidentally, that went for any and all new members of the team as well.

He thought he had made quite a commitment until she said, "Oh, wonderful" and tried to get off one of her "Dear Mom" letters again.

He told her to knock it off.

"You got it," she said. Then she pulled him closer and added: "Mmmmm, you smell nice, too, babe."